Love From Beyond

By Crissie Sinclair

Crissie Sinclair

Edited by Jane Hammett, Advanced Professional Member, Chartered Institute of Editing and Proofreading (CIEP)

Artwork inspired by Sally Peters, Upton upon Severn, Worcester.

Acknowledgements

I wish to thank all the friends and family that have helped me to write this book – in particular, Colin, who got me writing in the first place. Thanks to my mum, who kept me topped up with tea and encouragement. Many thanks to Jane Hammett, who edited this book. Also, thanks to Edie Baylis and Tracy N. Traynor, who helped with all the tricky formatting.

Table of Contents

Chapter 1

Where to begin? I could start by telling you about how William had lived, all the things he'd done, the people he met, his loves and losses. Instead I will start with the most important day: the day he died.

William had celebrated his seventeenth birthday just weeks before. Things had been good, but not that day. He had gone to bed early thinking he had yet another cold coming. The cut on his leg was annoying him too. He had been roused from sleep by the almost inhuman screams of his mother. Thoughts raced through his head as he stood and watched, dumbstruck, while his family cried and wailed over his cold, lifeless body. Yet here he stood, watching all of this unfold. The how and why would not be clear for many years.

The first few months after his death were by far the worst. His father cried very little, but buried himself in work. His mother, by contrast, cried all the time and seemed in a perpetual state of confusion. His younger brother and best friend,

John, turned to drink. At first glance, he appeared to be relatively happy, but he had always been a happy drunk. However, having spent the night drinking the inn dry he would sit in the main room talking to William, while the fire slowly turned to ash. William could only watch, frustrated by his inability to communicate with his family in any way. He watched their grief continue and their inability to cope with daily life dwindle. His anger grew with each setback they faced.

One day, William followed his father out towards the pigs. His father suddenly stopped, put his bucket down and rubbed his arms, as if he was cold. "I know you are there, son. But you can't stay here, you have to move on."

Horror filled William. He knew he was dead, but this was an insult that he hadn't seen coming. He and his brother had been supposed to inherit together. They had planned to raise their own children under the same roof. The brothers had such plans, yet here was William, receiving his marching orders from his own father! William walked round to face him, his fists clenched. Rage boiled in him and he prepared to give his father a piece of his mind, even if he couldn't hear him. When William saw his father's face, he was stunned. Tears flowed down his face, leaving telltale clean lines.

"We all love you, and we won't ever forget you, but for all our sakes and yours, don't stay here watching us grow old. We will see you soon enough, with whatever comes next. But for now, my boy, you must move on and try and find some peace. And maybe with time, so will we."

If William could have cried, he would have. Sadly, all he could do was try to put a hand on his father's shoulder, but it went right through. His father was right. Staying here wouldn't help anyone. It would be hard to leave, but at least he wouldn't have to pack. So far, the furthest horizon William had seen was the next town. Now, he could travel, see the world. Maybe get as far as London.

Had William lingered a few moments more and looked back at his father one last time, he would have seen him, a strong man, collapse in the pig pen. On his knees, his father hugged the ugly old sow, crying over the loss of his eldest son. The sow's expression remained nondescript, and she continued to chew a random piece of fodder.

William had instead moved inside to say goodbye to his mother, who stood staring at pieces of vegetable rise and fall in the bubbling stew pot. He attempted to kiss her on the cheek, but it didn't work. His brother was taking out his frustrations on the wood pile. He had always been a bit awkward with an axe, so just in case William just waved and walked off into the unknown.

Many years had passed before William found himself back in his home village of Bechford. He had been a lot further away than London. He had travelled the world and met so many ghosts, and watched so many people grow up and grow old. But he missed home. At first he had been almost scared to go home, in case his family had remained and become hellions. But now he longed to see his old house and town.

William was still dressed in the clothes he had been buried in: the simple woollen clothes of a fourteenth-century commoner. He wore a leather belt with a small pouch hanging from it, and an expensive pair of leather shoes. The shoes had been a birthday present from his family, just a few weeks before he had died. Burying him in his old shoes just felt wrong, his mother had said.

When he had left, Bechford had been a modest size, with a few small farms and a few houses. William's home was best described as a smallholding – just a few acres, but enough land to farm to feed them all through the winter, with a little to sell at market. Now the village was a bustling town, full of people, traffic and noise. He walked along the main road, recognising the odd old building hiding behind the new flashy facade. What had been the butcher's was now a mobile phone shop, advertising the latest models on offer. William lingered outside, admiring the clean, crisp interior through the window. To the living, everything in the street seemed normal. But there were two men dressed in traditional butchers' outfits, watching over all the comings and goings in the shop. The two men spotted William and waved cheerfully at him. He waved and smiled back, then he walked on through the melee.

Being ignored by the vast majority of living people gave William a sense of anonymity; the same was true of most of the dead, he supposed, but spending too long living like this – ignored, unseen – led to severe depression. Like so many other ghosts, William had preferred his own company in the first few years after his death. This meant that he had to fight off darker thoughts more than he would have liked. Not all the dead win this internal battle, but those who don't aren't generally talked about. Spiralling emotions, whether anger, grief or simply depression, can lead to unpleasant outcomes for the dead. But a genuine smile spread over William's face whenever someone stopped to say hello.

"Good day to you. I'm Felicia and this is my ward, Mark." The young woman smiled proudly at the baby in her arms.

"Good day to you both. I'm William; it's a pleasure to meet you," William responded gently, rubbing the boy's hand. Mark responded by chewing the silver teething ring he clutched in his tiny hands.

"Are you new to town?" she asked.

"No, not really, but it's been a while since I have been back."

Felicia's smile grew wider. "Then you must come to the meeting tonight, down by the old mill. Everyone will be there."

"That would be lovely. I'll see you there," said William. They both bowed slightly and continued in opposite directions.

Conversations like this are common among the dead. The rush of life is gone; getting to know someone can take decades, but that's alright. When you are dead, time is all you have. Meetings are also common; the dead need an excuse to get together. Without the need to eat or the ability to work, drink or even commute, finding others to talk to is important. The living might call it therapy or a gossip group, but the dead tended to just call them meetings.

The infectious smile that began when he saw Mark and Felicia would not go away. Without realising it, William smiled until he found himself at the end of his road. His expression was difficult to read. His heart sank, but he also felt buoyant.

The farm was gone, replaced by several pleasant detached houses, each with its own neat garden and drive. At the end of the road stood his house. It was far larger and grander now, but he knew it instinctively. It had been extended more than a few times, in both the traditional timber and brick, but in its heart it was the same as when he'd left it.

William recalled the house only having two rooms when he was little, then when his brother was a toddler, friends and neighbours came to extend it. Reaching the front gate, William looked back up the road, remembering how excited he had been as a small boy to see a horse pulling freshly downed tree trunks, ready to build their extension. A smile flickered back across his face, then his gaze dropped and the moment was gone.

William noticed the family as they left but continued round the property to the garden at the rear. In the dark of the noon sun he saw many changes, and yet some stark similarities. The herb garden was now a vegetable patch, but the field where William's family had grown most of their food had disappeared under houses and gardens. Over the fence to one side he could see the roof of a posh, but well-used, summer house. The orchard was gone, but William could still smell sweet apple blossom on the breeze.

Memories drifted through his mind as he wandered towards the pig sty. He placed a hand on the cool glass of the greenhouse that now stood in its place, hoping to connect with his last memory of the home he had once known. Sadly, nothing but stale, painful memories entered his mind. His family were all gone; he had lingered, but they had not. This wasn't some sort of spectral sense, but a gut instinct that William had learned to trust. William had mixed feelings about this. His existence could be very lonely and frustrating, and he wouldn't wish it on his loved ones. But to be able to speak to them or hold them one last time would make everything bearable.

At this point, I should explain a few things. Some people linger in this way, but not all. No one knows where the others go or what happens to those that eventually move on. Some things are best not known. What seems unbearable to the casual observer can become the norm when you find yourself having to live it. Other situations can appear to be a blessing, yet when the imagined becomes reality, you may find that reality isn't all it's cracked up to be.

Those who linger, inhabit a world flipped. When the living are enjoying the summer sun, the dead experience a cold midwinter night. When the living are bundled up tight against the icy blasts of winter, the dead are bathed in the hot summer sun. These differences take some getting used to, but given time, adjustments are made and it becomes normal to see snow falling over oblivious sunbathers. These differences aren't normally a problem until the dead have to go inside – away from the moonlight.

Unfortunately the dead can't change their clothes to suit the weather. A few have mastered the art of altering their appearance, but underneath they are still wearing what they were buried in. No one truly understands this phenomenon, but here are the facts: it's not what you die in that matters, it's what you are buried or cremated in. Very lucky for those who died swimming or even having sex! Instead, most are dressed in their Sunday best or a favourite outfit.

Of course, there are exceptions – in William's experience, those who are not dealt with properly. He had met several individuals over the years who had drowned at sea or fallen on the field of battle. He had heard of a former soldier whose body had been retrieved from a field in Ypres, years after the Great War. Then his bones had been dressed in a smart suit for reburial, rather than the tattered uniform he had died in. When his remains were placed inside a proper grave, his old uniform changed to the dress uniform the War Graves Commission had chosen. But this was a rare event and only known about by word of mouth.

The unconscious need for the living to carefully clean and dress a body for burial or cremation is unclear. Is it some sort of psychic link between the living and the dead? Or perhaps a result of evolution? If the latter is true, what came first? The act of cleaning or the dead's attire?

Those who had been cremated always carried the faint smell of a bonfire. For William, this brought back memories of burning the autumn leaves, mead in hand, his brother and father by his side, smiling in the warm glow of the open fire. A powerful tonic against the enclosing darkness of the coming winter. But the orchard was gone.

William left the garden and ventured inside the house. Even after the various extensions, William could still spot familiar things: the holes his brother had cut in the door frame to fit hinges remained, despite the absence of the heavy door they supported. William's room was small and only had space for a bed and a small cupboard; now it was an up-to-date utility room. The main room of William's house had served as living space, kitchen, and bedroom for his younger brother. This was now a large, bright kitchen that opened onto the garden. All very nice, he thought, but it's a shame the fireplace was gone. His father had sold his best goat to buy the stone to build it, and would be livid that it was gone. William walked past a bright dining room and into the main living room. To his surprise and joy, the fireplace stood there, in brilliant condition and obviously the focal point of the room. It was surrounded by large, sumptuous sofas. Rich curtains framed the windows, each of which had a beautiful view of the garden.

Even though the house was much bigger than it had been in William's day, it still managed to retain its homely feel. His mother might not have approved of all the décor, but she would have loved its overall feel. His mother had been seamstress for the lady of the manor, and spent all her spare time making things to improve their lives. Some people said it was a waste of time, but the whole family appreciated the cushions, rugs and curtains she made; they made their lives just that little bit softer and warmer.

Upstairs was similar, and yet not: each room expressed a different personality. He had only seen half of the upstairs when the current family returned. He walked through the next door and was instantly mesmerised by the chrome and glass of the luxurious bathroom. As he looked at his absent reflection, a woman entered. She stood beside William, ran the tap then patted cold water on her face. She glanced up at the mirror. "I don't know how much more I can take," she said, then turned rapidly and threw up in the toilet. William politely left as a teenage girl entered. As he passed through the teenager, he expected to feel the usual sensation – like someone walking over your grave – but it didn't happen this time. It felt more like an electric shock. Both of them felt it; they simultaneously stopped and inhaled deeply. But then it was gone.

William recognised the familiar symptoms of chemotherapy treatment and, being a gentleman, left the family to give them some privacy. The dead in general have great sympathy for the dying; it's a stark reminder of what their last days were like. Fighting the urge to offer words of comfort or advice can be overwhelming and impossible to suppress. For those close to the end, these sentiments can on occasion be heard. Whether they are heeded is always down to the individual. The dead do get a thrill when they recognise that someone has heard them and has taken on their words of wisdom.

Settling things properly eases the mind, leaving people free and calm. When the inevitable moment comes, the effort of those last breaths is something we will all have to contend with, sooner or later. But it isn't physical strength but your own inner strength that enables you to exhale, and not to panic, when you realise you are done.

The final thoughts we all have about what might come next aren't normally talked about, by either the living or the dead. It's fair to say that no one gets it completely right while they still have a pulse. If they did know for certain what came next, would they feel fear – or would it free their soul?

Chapter 2

When William had died, the mill was in its heyday. People would come every few days to meet and talk while their corn was ground. Oh, how times have changed! But the mill hadn't always been so popular. Giving up any of your crop was a no-no, then the women realised the benefits of leaving the daily grind to the miller. It gave them more time to do other work, making them more profitable and less tired.

Most of the users would stay outside, watching their bags being lifted magically up into the top of the building, before disappearing inside. They would then wait a while until a neat bag came out, filled with thoroughly milled corn. The whole process was the stuff of legend to most, but not to William and his brother. The miller was very proud of his craft, and more than willing to answer questions and to show people around. The two brothers always volunteered to take the corn to the mill, then they could follow its process through the various drops and grinding stones.

Since he had no children of his own, the miller was keen to pass on his knowledge, and even paid the boys to clean the water wheel. It was midsummer; he showed them how to hold the wheel and to make it safe, then the boys dived down and cleared the weed that slowed the machinery. The cold water was a blessing on that hot summer's day: it was tiring work, but more fun than working the fields. The miller's wife brought them a ploughman's lunch and mead, and when the workings were all clear the miller paid the boys with a large bag of milled corn. Their father would have been annoyed at them having a day playing in the stream, not toiling with him in the field, then he had seen the bag and realised the value of the work they had done.

"You need a trade," he would tell them. "If you don't, you'll end up like me, working the land, earning a pittance." He was right, and both brothers embraced every chance to learn. William had wanted to become a miller, but until then, he had continued to work the land with his father and mother, while learning all he could about the mill and how it all worked.

William's younger brother was stocky, despite being several years younger than William. He was a good foot taller than William: tall like their mother, but built like their father, large, rippled and toned. Any man would have been proud to have a physique like his. John used his stature to his advantage: he thrived at manual labour, but also relished the delicate work that being a blacksmith gave him. This was not just his trade, but his calling. His father's strength and his mother's finesse allowed him to create truly beautiful and functional pieces. The lord of the manor had commissioned him to create the ornate hinges and locks for the new part of the big house – something John always boasted about – and that in turn brought more trade to the smithy.

William, by contrast, was of average height and slightly built, but this hid his strength. As a child he was bullied for being small, but when he was challenged to test his strength against the older boys, he nearly always won. His dark hair was a stark contrast to his light blue eyes. He wasn't overly handsome, but his eyes beautifully expressed his kind, light-hearted nature. He might not have had the chiselled jaw some women find attractive, but he possessed the best of personalities, which made him very attractive to all those around him. His crowning feature was his smile. His smile beamed from his whole face, broad and open. His eyes frequently smiled with his mouth. Given his general temperament, this meant he smiled a lot. Especially at the local girls…

William turned a bend in the stream and saw how the years had treated the once beautiful mill. The wheel had long gone; so too had the roof and most of the walls. The once pristine mill had now fallen, and nature had taken most of it back. He stood and took it all in. The miller and his wife would have been disappointed by the sight, and yet they too would be able to see the beauty in its current state. The sublime grace of the plants growing up, through and over the walls, in a mass of vivid greens, with accents of colour blossoming here and there, attracting a multitude of butterflies and bees. An air of peace and tranquillity encapsulated the area – a stark contrast to the hustle of its former life.

The stream still flowed past the building, now free to bypass the now non-existent water wheel. No longer forced to work such heavy machinery or constrained by man-made channels, the water seemed to take on a gentler attitude and sound. For water is truly eternal; it can't be broken or beaten into submission, only coerced into change. No matter how well you build, how hard the stone is, water will always win. Whether it's the slow wearing down that takes aeons, or the fast, thunderous force of a flash flood, water will always be victorious.

"You made it. Most people are here," said Felicia. Mark was busy examining the grass. With determination, he reached for a dandelion and yanked it out. William bent down to speak to him, and Mark thrust the dandelion and stray blades of grass into his hand. Then William's knee became the perfect anchor for Mark to pull himself up on.

Holding on tightly to William's trousers, Mark stood proudly, but with a slight wobble.

"I'll introduce you."

"Thank you," replied William, as Felicia removed Mark from William's leg. Dead babies are unusual. Dead children are more common, but invariably they creep everyone out. It's not anything you can put your finger on; it's just wrong on so many levels to see a young life cut short. With no limitations or parents to guide them, dead children normally 'go wrong', as most would put it. But when they start down that path, they generally don't last long and sort of burn out. To meet a happy dead child was truly rare, and gave William's soul a real lift. Mark was a very special baby indeed. Felicia was dressed like a Victorian nanny. William didn't need this to be confirmed; he could see from the way she looked after Mark that it wasn't just a job to pay the bills, but a strong maternal instinct that paid her more than any amount of money.

Felicia was as good as her word, and introduced William to everyone in turn. While people talked about themselves and the news of the day, Mark was free to roam, climbing up different people and launching himself from lap to lap. Each person talked to him as if he could understand everything, and in fairness he laughed and gurgled at the appropriate moments. William had no idea how long he had been lingering; it was more than possible that he did in fact have the intelligence of an adult. This could lead to madness, but Mark seemed content with his existence.

William was introduced to the two butchers from the phone shop.

"Hello, my name is Ethan and this is Tom."
"That's Thomas, how many times do I have to tell you?"

William shook both of their hands and they began to talk about the fall of the high street to bland monochrome chain stores. The two men appeared to be enemies, yet neither seemed prepared to leave their former home. They both wore white overalls, a striped apron and a straw boater. They looked so similar, they might as well have been brothers. Luckily one was taller than the other, so there was an easy way to distinguish them.

"We would generally shout at each other all day while the shop was empty, but business is business, and these young upstarts have no idea what they are doing, so we agree to hate each other, but to work together for the sake of the shop," said Ethan. Thomas nodded in agreement.

"Without us, the shop would have failed ages ago," said Thomas. This time Ethan nodded in agreement. Even though they had been born many years apart, they behaved like quarrelling brothers – each jealous of the other, yet both driven by the same ambition.

As they walked towards a group of elderly people, Felicia whispered with a smile, "All Thomas and Ethan do is dust; they haven't mastered any other skill. But they're still convinced they help."

The names of the three elderly men and one woman left William's mind as soon as they had entered. He had met people like them before: they would linger long enough to see their spouses join them, then they would move on together. They were all very polite and wanted to know what the town had been like in his day. William, of course, obliged, but only got as far as describing the mill in its heyday before Felicia "had" to introduce him to the others.

Next came a young man, mid-twenties at most, and obviously a rocker in his day, going by his leather jacket and Brylcreemed quiff.

"Nat, this is William. William, may I introduce Nat?"

Nat swung his hand in wide to shake William's hand. While he patted William's upper arm with his other hand, he eyed the small pouch on his belt. "Alright, man? Welcome to the neighbourhood."

"Nice to meet you."

"I'm guessing you've been round the block a few times," said Nat, looking at William's dated outfit.

"A few times. You?" replied William as they leaned against the remnants of a wall. Felicia went to check on Mark, leaving them free to talk.

"A little, but I bow to superior knowledge. I hear you died here. Has much changed?"

"Quite a bit, and yet very little is actually different."

Silence fell between them as a pretty young lady crept past them. She looked up briefly and smiled. Both men smiled back, and Nat waved at her.

"That's Claire – she doesn't talk much. She's only been here a few years. She'll settle in soon," explained Nat, looking nervously at the floor.

"You do know death doesn't last forever. You should just go talk to her."

Nat smiled and shuffled anxiously. William had hit a nerve. "She wasn't smiling at me."

"I think she was. You've got everything to gain, and at worst you'll get a slap. Worth a try. I'll test the waters for you," said William, clapping Nat playfully on the shoulder and walking off towards Claire. Nat didn't have time to object.

"Hello, I'm William. Are you Claire?"

"Yes."

"Everyone seems very welcoming."

Claire nodded.

"Nat is very friendly. And he was right about you."

"What did he say about me?"

"That you were quiet but beautiful. I think he could do with someone to talk to who's on his wavelength."

Claire gave a bigger smile. The two stood in silence, listening to the others chatting.

"Does anyone know how Amber is?" asked Thomas.

"Her daughter was in the other day. She looked tired, poor thing," replied Ethan.

"Where do they live?" asked one of the elderly men.

"Orchard Farm House," Felicia chimed in. William's ears perked up. That was the name of his old house.

"Excuse me." Smiling at Claire, William turned and joined the others. "I think I saw her earlier – they live in my old house. It looks like she's having chemo."

"I heard Luke, her husband, saying she was going for another round. But sadly it looks like it's terminal. I hate seeing the living suffer like this; it's not fair."

Everyone nodded in agreement with the little old lady. Then they all looked towards William.

"I know you're only just back, but would you stand watch?" said Felicia quietly.

"They are in my old house; it makes it my responsibility," replied William. There was a lump in his throat.

Standing watch was always a hard thing to do, but it was the duty of the dead to try to help the dying. William had done this many times before. It was an invasion of their privacy, but it had to be done. Deciding who would stand watch was normally done jointly at meetings like this.

William left the meeting feeling daunted by the task that lay before him, but he had a job to do, and this task mattered to the dead. He would shoulder this responsibility with grace and dignity, if possible.

Amber continued the chemotherapy, but to no avail. Only a few weeks after William had met her, she had changed dramatically. The weight had fallen off her, she no longer had the energy to leave her bed, and even the thought of putting on make-up or her wig seemed to exhaust her.

William was struck by her smile; it was always there behind her eyes. Only when she was alone would it slip, and her fear of what was coming would become evident for anyone to see. During these quiet moments, William tried to reassure her. "Whatever happens, you won't be alone. You will always have family around you. Blood doesn't make you family, it's what's in your heart that matters, and yours is full of love, so please don't worry."

No matter how much William talked or tried to make himself known to her, Amber remained oblivious to this thoughtful spirit guiding her through her last days. Soon enough, Amber was being seen twice daily by the district nurses, the doctor was calling at least once a day, and the

Macmillan team had been to see if they could help with her hospice care. Despite taking heavy doses of painkillers, she remained in pain, unable to eat properly, but her smile still shone out.

In between visits from family, friends and professionals, the family tried to spend quiet time with her, talking about everything from who had posted what on Facebook to what was happening in the wider world. Certain conversations were reserved for when it was just Amber and her daughter Sarah. The two of them talked about her will, the funeral, and how Sarah would look after her father and younger brother, Oliver. Conversations like these could be deeply upsetting for all those involved, including William, but there could be an element of humour involved, even if it was simply choosing one of the songs from a list of the worst songs to play at a cremation. The favourite was 'Another One Bites the Dust' by Queen – it is a classic, after all. And definitely a better choice than the *Countdown* theme tune.

Amber's husband Luke filled his days with practical things, despite everything: he prepared three square meals a day, all of them well balanced and healthy. The house was spotless, he had found a great website that had taught him how to do everything properly, from cleaning the bathroom to making the oven look like new. In his mind he was showing his wife that he could do everything and could manage without her, but it didn't help. Amber worried that he would burn out sooner rather than later. Luke worried that there weren't step-by-step instructions for the truly difficult things, like helping your children watch their mother slowly die.

With each new housekeeping skill he mastered, the cat seemed to get more and more nervous, as though he would be next on the list of things that needed to be cleaned and sterilised. William and the cat seemed to get on well. Wherever he went, the cat followed him, purring and curling up next to him as soon as he sat down. This friendliness towards William was the complete opposite of his behaviour towards Luke, who he subjected to bouts of hissing and sly scratches.

As always in these situations, the ones that suffer the most are those who are left behind. The younger they are, the deeper the impact. Sarah had many close friends, but even they bought into the lie that she was coping okay. Yet in the middle of the night William would find himself sitting on the end of her bed, watching as she silently sobbed into her pillow. Occasionally he'd try to offer her comfort.

William regularly got visits from the dead. Meetings for him were out of the question at the moment, as he stood watch twenty-four hours a day. He was on hand at all times. Nat came to see William the most, invariably smiling and glowing, thanks to his new relationship with Claire. They had held hands but not kissed yet – this was a massive step forward after nearly twenty years of just saying hello and glancing at each from afar. Nat's happiness was a necessary boost for William during his term of duty.

Each visitor to William would stay outside to bring him up to date on other matters, then William would show them upstairs, so they could pay their respects to Amber. Some would kiss her on the forehead while others talked to her, offering their own comforting or insightful words. Felicia spent hours just sitting, trying to hold her hand, saying nothing, just smiling at Amber as she slept fitfully. During this time William took Mark on a tour of the house and garden, carefully pointing out all of the changes, and telling the child stories of what had happened when he and his family had lived there. William relished this time away from his duties. It was difficult to tell if Mark was content; he always seemed happy with his lot.

The only thing that all the dead visitors did was to sit in the same chair. Oddly enough, this chair seemed to be avoided by living visitors; it remained empty even when the room was filled with people standing awkwardly around the bed. The only person who sat in this chair was Sarah. Did she know that William or his visitors always stood up to allow her to sit, or was she just unaware of the feelings that everyone else experienced around the chair?

Amber's family tried their best to make sure she wasn't left on her own for too long, but when she was, William was there, sitting quietly in case he could help. During the long, slow hours of the night, Amber would lie and stare at the chair in which William and the others sat, not saying anything, just staring at the empty chair, surrounded by darkness. During this time William would describe his life and death. Detailed and convoluted trains of thoughts on how the house and village had changed made up large portions of these one-sided conversations. Amber never once responded. But that didn't matter; what mattered was that he was here if she needed him.

"Do you want some tea?" asked Sarah.

"No thanks, just some water please," Amber replied.

Sarah left and quickly returned from the bathroom with a fresh glass of cool water. Placing it within easy reach of her mother, she asked, "Anything else I can get you or do for you? We could just sit and watch TV."

Amber shook her head. "I'm fine. I'll just have a doze for a bit. Besides, I have my guardian angel watching me." To William's shock, she turned towards him, smiled and gently closed her eyes for the last time. He had been heard by some folk who were dying, but he had never been seen. This was a moment of pride for him, but it was tinged with sadness that she would soon pass from this world. A few hours later, her family by her side, she slipped peacefully away. Standing at the back of the room were William, Felicia and Mark, all in sombre silence. Even the normally exuberant Mark remained quiet. Words of comfort came solely from the family now; nothing William could say would make any difference.

They waited for the flash.

Amber slowly let go of her last breath, then it happened. A blinding white flash filled the room, and shards of light so bright they appeared solid exploded out of every window and door of the house. This beacon stretched endlessly outwards, telling all the dead nearby that Amber had passed on and not stayed to join their motley crew. This wave went unnoticed by the living, but to the dead it was unmissable. Its force nearly blew the three of them off their feet, but it also filled them with an overwhelming sense of love and warmth. These powerful feelings, combined with their own relief, gave them a high that lasted several hours and kept them all smiling for several days. No one would want to linger, as they had.

You might think that with Amber's passing William's watch would be over, but he stayed in order to keep an eye on her family. With her death, the whole family was finally able to cry properly and openly for the first time, except Sarah. She cried a little with her brother and father, but every night she sobbed silently into her pillow, in an unconscious effort to shield the others from her grief.

Luke's new-found status as a domestic god failed in dramatic fashion. No one was hungry, so he stopped cooking, and all the cleaning stopped. His focus was on the funeral, nothing else. Grief and gloom encapsulated the house and its occupants. Anything that could bring the slightest glimmer of joy to them seemed to be banned. Music of any sort, regardless of its upbeat tempo, caused tears to flow, apparently without end. Their favourite TV shows were abandoned, and screens remained as black as their own inner turmoil. Throughout all of this, William continued to provide his own brand of support to the family. His efforts went unnoticed by all except the cat, who stuck to William even more than before, but now without his telltale purr. Grief had become so infectious in this house that even the cat was affected.

Finally, the day of the funeral came. William hoped that this would bring some closure to this suffering family, and their grief could start to lift. Family and friends descended on the house like flies, offering condolences and hugs, in preparation for the moment when they would say goodbye for the last time. With all the hustle and bustle, it took William a while to notice that Sarah was absent. She was upstairs in her room. She was dressed in her best gothic clothes, brightened with a single rose from the garden. She stood in front of a full-length, free-standing mirror trying to put on her make-up, which in William's humble opinion was perfect. With the final touches done she began to cry again, causing her eyeliner and mascara to run.

"Just leave your eyes and wear sunglasses," said William. He couldn't give her a hug, which was what she obviously needed, but only a hug from her mother could have stopped her overwhelming sadness.

"Fuck!!" Sarah screamed, throwing a bottle of foundation at the mirror, smashing it to pieces.

The sombre silence of the house was broken. People quickly arrived at her door, asking what had happened and if she was okay. Amber's younger sister Paige arrived too. She said nothing to Sarah, but set about removing everyone from the room and closing the door. Sarah had collapsed to the floor in tears; Paige sat in front of her. She gently pushed Sarah's hair back from her face and started to remove the offending make-up. Then she reapplied foundation, not eye make-up, then went to search the room, still not saying anything. Paige returned to Sarah with a pair of sunglasses and put them on her face. "There, all sorted. You're just missing one thing…" She pulled a fresh packet of tissues from her pocket and placed them in Sarah's hand. Without letting go, she helped Sarah off the floor and onto her feet.

"Go and get some fresh air and clear your head. I'll sort this" Paige said, indicating the shards of broken mirror that littered the floor. Sarah did as she was told and headed to the garden. William remained to watch Aunt Paige.

"Thank you, that was just what she needed. I hope you can help them more than I can."

Paige continued to clean carefully as William left the room to check on the others. A smile passed across Paige's face as she realised that this simple act of kindness had helped Sarah on such a horrific day.

At the funeral, everyone – family, friends and the dead – stood in silence as the service took place.

Readings by family and friends reduced most of the congregation to tears; even the dead were wiping their eyes, most remembering their own funerals. But they stayed standing guard at the end of the pews. Then came the procession out to the funeral plot and the slow descent of the coffin, to the sound of tears, sobs and the vicar's eulogy. The living and the dead then took turns to say their goodbyes, after which they all wandered off. The dead were keen to usher the exhausted William back to the mill for a well-earned rest.

Chapter 3

The living recover their strength by eating and sleeping, two things the dead cannot do; instead they spend time with water. Not dull, lifeless water that has been forced to travel through pipes, pumps and turbines in order to provide drinking water, or water that comes from fountains, but raw water. Whether it's gentle or forceful, a stream, river or the sea, it is untamed and unmastered. It flows freely, binding all of us together, and provides the dead with a constant source of energy. Water is truly magical in this regard: even the living get a noticeable lift after visiting water like this or after experiencing a powerful storm. The living might see this as a temporary psychological boost, but to the dead it is real and tangible, and part of daily life. The dead require the energy boost that water gives them, and must top up periodically if they are to avoid burning out.

Over the next few weeks William remained, as instructed, at the mill, or close to the stream and its healing properties. Most nights, the dead also returned to comply with their duties: to help with William's recovery. The long dark days were his own. During this time he sat and listened to the bees buzzing in the long grass and the blissful sound of birds flitting through the trees. Although it seemed weird at first to hear this myriad of life in the dark, it acted as a powerful sedative, letting his mind wander and relax. Well, that was the idea. However, William couldn't stop wondering how the family was, and if Sarah was still crying every night.

The meetings became monotonous. The most common topic of discussion was the plans to build more houses on the other side of town, and the loss of yet another bank, and how this would impact on the businesses that were already struggling to beat back the tidal wave of online services. Needless to say, these conversations were led by the butchers. Both became quite animated on the subject, and were not afraid to make their opinions known. These heated exchanges were a welcome distraction for William. Worrying about bigger issues made his own concerns fade into the background, if only for a little while.

William was able to take immense joy from the blossoming relationship between Nat and Claire. The two of them had quickly become inseparable, either holding hands or glancing subtly at each other when they weren't physically joined. Nat was happy to join William, away from the others, to talk about the simple things in death, such as which film they should go and see when William was better, but he always kept one eye on Claire. Claire talked more, but it was the change in her confidence that William noticed most. She no longer smiled and looked at the floor; instead, she held people's gaze and smiled. As her confidence grew, she glowed, something that seemed to magnetise Mark to her, and the two of them spent many happy hours together, in among the grass and flowers.

Standing guard for so long had taken all of William's strength. Being at the mill acted like an IV drip. After several weeks of being too weak to move anywhere, except from one broken piece of wall to another, William slowly but surely found that he was able to venture further from the life support of the stream. After a couple of months, he finally felt able to go back to the house. The change he found was dramatic, to say the least. The weight of grief that had so affected all of the inhabitants had lifted. In its place was normal family life, but with a noticeable gap.

William had got to the house just before the break of dawn. The songbirds belted out their joy at the beginning of a new day and the end of the cold, dark night. For William it was dusk, but that didn't matter. While he stood guard, he had become accustomed to moving around the house in pitch darkness. Up and down the street, lights flickered on as the living woke up and began to start their day. In William's house it was no different: for this scarred family, like everyone else, winter was rapidly approaching. The dull green of the trees was gone, replaced by the vibrant colours of autumn. Plants and animals were preparing for the dormant months of winter, by hiding away from the icy wind and rain of a typical British winter.

In the garden, birds flocked to the feeders, emptying them before a single human had stepped out into the day. Fallen leaves lay everywhere, providing shelter to insects and acting as a natural blanket to the plants that had started to die back. For the dead, the autumn months felt like spring, with the weather getting warmer and the nights getting noticeably shorter. In the garden, the only plant that seemed to be on the same wavelength to the dead was the holly, whose berries had started to ripen as the cold started to bite. This angry tree, with all its thorny spikes, provided shelter for so many, and a vital food source. Given the way the noisy starlings fought over the best berries, they must be tasty indeed. William had tried one when he was little. Despite its alluring appearance, he found the berry to be bitter and totally unpalatable to a human. In the fading light of the dead's day, William was drawn to the holly's vibrant colours and its come-and-have-a-go attitude to the impending bleakness.

His visit was supposed to be a brief one, but as he watched the family having breakfast, he felt he had to stay longer. Father and son seemed to be doing well, as they were back to their normal routine. They appeared to be happy, discussing everyday things, but there was a stillness to Sarah that unnerved William. This young woman had been vivacious and full of life, but in the early morning light, and despite her well-applied make-up, she just looked tired.

William's sense of concern for this vulnerable woman was overwhelming. But how could he help, since she was totally unaware that he existed?

As the family left for school and work, William's desire to stay was suddenly and quite unexpectedly brought to an end as his knees buckled and his head began to swim. Exhaustion was taking over again. He would have to return to the mill sooner rather than later.

William waited quietly in the house, moving slowly from room to room. He hoped that in the faint light of the dead moon some solution to the problem that now overwhelmed his thoughts might present itself, but to no avail. He knew that Sarah was struggling mentally, and he wanted desperately to help her, but he didn't know how. The surroundings looked familiar and reassuring: photos had not changed, the house remained in a clean but lived-in condition, nothing was out of place, but there was something there … if only he could find it. It took William a few hours to make his way upstairs. By that time, moonlight streamed into one side of the house through the open curtains. Luckily, the bedrooms he wanted to see were on this side. The family bathroom, spare room and Oliver's room were too dark for him to make out anything beyond the doorway. Inside these rooms the darkness took on a life of its own, almost solid in structure, yet never-ending in depth, and not quite as still as you would like it to be.

"Discretion is the better part of valour," he said to himself as he ventured further down the hall.

The bathroom was unlikely to hold any clues. Oliver seemed to have bounced back well, and the spare room only contained the basics for visiting guests and a cupboard full of boxes filled with random things, such as school reports and old china that no longer belonged to a set. William knew that as soon as he was able, he would have to get back, so he had to spend his time wisely. Despite this, he found himself loitering in Amber and Luke's bedroom. Having spent so much time in here, he felt comfortable and at ease. As with the rest of the house, this room appeared to be unchanged in general. William was only able to discern subtle changes. The piles of medication that had been stacked on the dressing table had been cleared. In their place stood a selection of family photos. The smell of disinfectant and hand sanitiser had been replaced by the sweet smell of lavender that emanated from a reed diffuser on the bedside table. Yet the rest of the furnishings had not moved.

Exhaustion hit William afresh, and he found himself sitting back in the chair. Absently, he stared at the empty bed. Memories poured into his mind – but not, as you might expect, the morbid, depressing times of Amber's final breath or the yelps of discomfort she gave as she rolled from one painful side of her body to the other. Instead he found himself smiling at his memories of Amber and her children playing a game of snap, play-fighting, or the sight of the cat trying – and failing miserably – to jump onto the bed, and the ensuing withering look the cat gave to all those who had dared to laugh at his mistiming and subsequent embarrassment. It's these beautifully simple memories that carry you forward and hold you up when you need them, not the impact of a wedding or the birth of a baby. It's the small, easily missed moments from within the larger experiences that have the greatest impact. Not the wedding vows, but who catches the bouquet after launching themselves at it. It's the sensation of cutting the umbilical cord, not the hours of sweating, swearing and contractions. No one really talks about these snippets of time, but when you remember the big things, they are always made up of tiny pieces that create the whole and give it an overall feeling. When William thought over his one-sided relationship with Amber, it was with joy and respect, not regret at her passing.

Finally William dragged himself away from the security of Amber and Luke's bedroom and tentatively crossed the threshold into Sarah's bedroom. If he had a pulse, it would have quickened as his anxiety from his invasion of her privacy affected his whole body. As it was, his hands shook with anticipation, while his stomach turned uncontrollably with guilt.

Nothing had changed in this room either. The empty frame of the broken mirror remained in place; the small shards that littered the edge had not been touched. The pieces that had shattered over the floor were nowhere to be seen, as Paige had promised. William lowered himself slowly to his knees so that he could look closely at the remains. Due to the dim light, feel was his best sense. At first he felt the soft bounce of the deep pile carpet, but as his hands moved gingerly towards the mirror's feet, he felt a hard space in among the bushy carpet fibres, where the mirror's feet had once stood. The mirror had been moved a few inches, but no more – had this been Paige clearing up? Had Sarah then moved the frame back for some reason – and, if so, why?

Why had Sarah kept the useless frame of the mirror? Was it important to her for some reason? The answer was here, but William couldn't quite put his finger on it. The mirror and the death of Sarah's mother were obviously connected somehow, but how? What William didn't know was that Sarah's grandmother had taught her to do her hair in front of this mirror, and had then left the mirror to her. Her grandmother didn't have much to leave. By the time Sarah was born, she was living in a nursing home, where she had thrived, living until Sarah was five.

With no other obvious clues to follow, William dragged himself back downstairs and collapsed onto the sofa. His body was exhausted, but his mind spun in circles. How could he help Sarah? She had done so much for her family, yet here she was still in the full throes of grief, while they had picked themselves up and were beginning to get used to their new reality.

William slumped on the sofa for several minutes, pondering how and what should happen next. Should he interfere? Grief, after all, is a personal thing, unique to everyone. The time it takes to complete the various stages varies from person to person, with individuals reacting differently and unpredictably. There was only one sensible thing to do: he would ask the others for their advice, and go from there.

One by one the family returned home from school and work. Their evening was fairly normal. Oliver did his homework in the dining room with his father's help, while Sarah prepared supper for them all. The pasta bake looked untidy, but it smelled wonderful and made William long to taste food once more. The family was settling down to eat when William realised that the dead sun was rising and his path home would be lit by the light of the dead's daytime. In his current state of tiredness, walking anywhere in the dark was not a good idea. In the past he had tried, but he always ended up bashing into something. He had been unaware of car alarms until he had fallen off a kerb and set one off by accident. The noise and his embarrassment had taught him a valuable lesson: the dead have all the time in the world, so why spend it walking into things? He knew that he could master the ability to touch things, if he worked hard. Typically, it only worked when he least expected or wanted it, which William found extremely frustrating.

Chapter 4

After resting at the house, William slowly made his way back to the mill.

"Why do you think she needs help?" asked Felicia after he had told her what he had seen.

"I don't know. There's just something not right. After all these years I trust my gut," replied William.

"But you've finished your watch, you've done your duty – what more can you do?" questioned Nat.

"You should always follow your instincts," said an older lady without looking up from her knitting. "It's why you have them."

"What can you do? Can she hear you?" asked Nat.

"I've been heard in the past, but not for a good long while, and only by one of the dying. So, I don't know how to communicate with her."

"You need to go to the haunted house. You need to practise," said Felicia.

The decision was made. First, William needed to get stronger, then he had to brush up on his skills as a ghost. Nat would go with William for moral support. The others would go about their own business and leave William to his self-imposed quest.

In every village, town and city you will find at least one building that's rumoured to be haunted. The best buildings, from the dead's perspective, are found near water and are run professionally by the dead. Their local house was upstream of the mill, and still run by a former master of the house. William met him when he first passed. He was a stern but fair man, much like the master who had employed William's brother John.

In this house, learning was key. Taking advantage was not allowed, and anyone showing signs of burning out would be dismissed and not allowed to return until they could show that they had a handle on things. Few establishments were so well run, as William had learned to his detriment.

"Relax. This is going to be fun. It's been ages since I came up here," said Nat as he bounced alongside William.

"I just hope the old man is still in charge. Without him, this place could be dangerous," William replied.

"Haunted houses aren't dangerous; they just scare the living."

"No, they don't. I've been to one before. Bugger scaring the living – I was terrified! You don't know how good you have it here," said William.

"If you say so, but I doubt it was that bad," said Nat.

Finally, the house came into view around a corner.

"I'd forgotten how magnificent it is – and they've done more work to it. Not bad, not bad at all," said William. Nat merely nodded in agreement.

As they got closer, William's nerves disappeared and excitement took over. "My brother made that door; I can't believe it's still here. Wow! It looks like someone has repaired a few bits, but it's still in great shape." William ran his hands over the aged wood and the intricate metalwork that flowed over it. He stood back to get a proper look, smiled at the handiwork, then walked through the closed door with a spring in his step. Nat followed.

The two spirits walked into the grand entrance hall. Dark wood panelling covered every wall. Due to the vast size of the space they were in, the walls felt miles away. To their right stood the staircase, which wound its way up three floors. Standing at the bottom, Nat looked straight up to the vast glass ceiling above. Daylight shone in, illuminating the space, revealing the finer details of the carved panelling. Old-fashioned silver gas sconces with modern electric bulbs lined the walls, adding to the overall feeling of the hall.

While Nat was engrossed in the ceiling, William put his head through some doors to see if anyone was around.

The dead master of the house appeared in the corridor, a smile on his face. "Welcome back, William, it's been too long," said the master, shaking William's hand warmly.

"It's good to be back. How are you? Still running things, I see," replied William.

"Someone has to keep things going. Nat, my boy, how are you?"

"Very well, sir, thank you." Nat and the master shook hands and Nat bowed slightly.

"So, what can I do for you both?" asked the master.

"William has a problem, and needs to brush up on his skills."

"I see. Well, we will have to see what you've learned since you left."

"I wasn't the best pupil, but I have got my anger under control, I think," William said.

"Follow me and we will see what can be done." The master of the big house had always been referred to as 'the master' when he was alive. This title, and the staff's respect for him, had not died with their deaths. The master had died before William had been born, but the years had had no impact on the man. He still stood tall and strong. He exuded power – but only wielded it when absolutely necessary.

He was so old that no one knew his name; some believed that he himself had forgotten it. But the dead always addressed him as 'sir' or 'master', regardless. Without knowing exactly when he had died, it was impossible to say whether he was tall, short or average for his time. To the modern eye, the master was of average height and build. He had a stern look about him, but the twinkle in his eye gave a glimpse of the true man behind the title.

William and Nat dutifully followed the master as he led them down to the dark cellars, lighting their way with an oil lamp. After passing a maze of empty corridors and unused room, the three entered what had been the kitchens. Even though they were underground and had been unloved for decades, light still entered through large windows mounted high above the vast rusting range. In the centre of the room still stood a long table, presumably too big to move or even rehouse. Scattered around the room were a multitude of boxes and random items left to collect dust. The only signs of life were the footprints of the odd wandering mouse looking for somewhere to nest. To the casual observer, all was still and dead.

The sun's rays moved slowly round the room as the master put William and Nat through their paces. The exercises started simple but quickly became more and more complex. They started with moving things. Both were able to blow and move some of the mountains of dust. Walking and making their steps heard proved more problematic. When William tried, only every other step could be heard by the living. To William, though, his steps seemed to echo, even though there was no echo in this room.

"Remember, you have to want the effect, while remaining calm and still. Concentrate harder, but don't force it," repeated the master time and again.

The two paced up and down, their posture and walks getting more and more ridiculous. Stamping, marching and even something akin to Monty Python's silly walks were tried, but the results were still random and inconsistent.

"Have you ever been able to touch someone? I know that was what you wanted to learn before," said the master.

"Never. But the one person I wanted to feel my touch is long since dead." William's mind and heart sank into his memories of holding his mother's hand. The hardest part of saying goodbye to his mother was not being able to kiss her cheek, as he had done so many times before.

"It's about time you learned, then. But we will need a live specimen," said the master. "Come on. The eldest has just turned eighteen. The poor boy is probably still drunk." The master smiled, then stood and left the room.

For the dead, hurting the living is a definite no-no. By all means you can play pranks on them, but never hurt or upset them in any way. When they manage to really upset, shock or even hurt the living, the dead can get an emotional high. Becoming addicted to this will lead to the dead burning out. The energy boost from strong emotional living people generally feels like being near water. However, the darker emotions that humans all feel have a greater impact on the dead – not just in terms of energy, but also at a mental level. Feeling genuine compassion for an individual who is in need prevents the dead from going into a downward spiral of spiritual depression.

Playing a prank on someone can have two outcomes: either they are scared, and the dead laugh, or the dead and the living laugh, sharing the moment. The first outcome leads to a powerful negative energy boost for the ghost, which can be highly addictive and will damage the ghost's soul. The latter will always give a positive energy boost to both the living and the dead.

William had managed to play a few pranks in his time. He had found that setting it up was the hardest part. One winter's night, William had stumbled upon several boys camping in a field. One of them started telling ghost stories – a point of both pride and humour to most of the dead. The other boys seemed to be really scared: they were old enough to camp alone, yet young enough to still want the comfort of their mother's hug.

The boy finished the story, making the others jump and yell in surprise. While he laughed at their response, William rubbed his hands with glee. He lay down at the boy's feet and waited. After a few minutes the boy moved and the hem of his trousers billowed slightly, opening a gap between his leg and the fabric. William closed his eyes and blew straight up his trouser leg. The boy who, moments before, had been taking the mick out of the others for being "little girls" now screamed loudly and jerked his body away from the sudden cold blast shooting up his leg.

All the boys laughed and giggled at the truly girly scream emitted by this so-called young man.

"I thought it was a bug!" he explained. "But it was just a draught." Checking his trouser leg for any insects, he continued to chuckle to himself, while William and the others laughed at how this brave boy had been brought down to the same level as the rest.

Most people have been on the end of something like this. Something happens, and you just laugh it off and forget about it. And for the most part, whatever happened was not caused by the dead. It was just the wind, or gravity, or something of that nature. But not all the time...

The joy of the boys laughing, including William, gave them all a much-needed boost to their mood and energy. But William had never intended to hurt or upset the boy, merely to bring him down a peg or two, and to get them all laughing.

Touching someone is the next step. But it's far more perilous. Most living people who feel a hand on their shoulder that isn't there would be terrified, and rightly so. But in the right moment, in the right situation, putting a hand on a shoulder will have the opposite effect. Rather than instilling fear, it can bring comfort or even strengthen the living.

For the dead, being noticed in any way was what they all wanted – but not to the detriment of the living. Being isolated and unnoticed in a room full of people is one of the most soul-destroying things that life – or death – has to offer. It is for these reasons the dead have meetings: so that they can be listened to and to interact with others.

All these thoughts passed through William's mind as they entered the bedroom. Through the thin curtains, the light revealed a scene of chaos. Four days earlier, Adam had turned eighteen. A brilliant day and night for him, followed by the hangover from hell. Last night, since it was Saturday, he had been out with yet more friends to celebrate his coming of age.

Adam lay face down across his bed, an arm touching the floor, one shoe on, one shoe off. His trousers were undone, but still on, and his T-shirt was somehow still attached to one arm only. Given the decibels of his snores, they could have set off a fire alarm next to him and he wouldn't notice or care.

The three dead stood and chuckled at Adam.

"I told you – he's still drunk. He won't notice a thing."

"Isn't he off to uni?" asked Nat.

"Yes. He needs to get used to drinking before he goes. He is improving. His mum put him to bed with a bucket and glass of water on his birthday. At least he attempted it himself this time."

"And one shoe off is better than needing Mum to help," said Nat. All three smiled, having all experienced similar nights when they were alive.

"Right, let's get on with it. I just hope he isn't too drunk. He needs to at least flinch, so we know it's worked." The master slowly reached down and gently touched the tip of Adam's nose. Adam rubbed his face and mumbled something about squashed frogs.

"Perfect. He's responsive but oblivious," said the master as he stood back, allowing William and Nat to take their positions on either side of the bed. They bent forward and smiled. This was a naughty but nice moment. Trying to tickle someone while remaining completely calm and focused is not easy.

The two tried desperately to make the young man move. For several minutes they focused on touching his bare flesh, but to no avail. The longer they tried, the more they smiled. Just the smell of the alcohol coming off Adam was intoxicating – even to the dead, it seemed. Without warning, Adam's arm twitched.

"I got one!" shouted Nat as he started to celebrate his victory.

"No, it was just a moth," said the master.

"Sorry, mate. Look – there it goes," said William, pointing at a small moth flapping round Adam's head.

"Damn."

"Keep trying. Remember, you have to want it, without forcing it," said the master.

Their smiles faded as the two ghosts became more frustrated at their inability to touch Adam. After ten minutes or so, they were exhausted from concentrating. William paced around the room, his hands on his head.

The master could see their frustration and suggested they have a break. "Let's go and rest. He's going to be in this state for a while. We can try again tomorrow."

The three spent the dark hours of the dead night lounging by the stream, trying to move the small pebbles that lay idly around them.

"If you want to be noticed, you have to master these basics. Touching someone is simple when you don't want to do it. We've all walked through someone, but when you want to touch them, that's a different thing entirely," the master explained.

"I can move things when I'm not thinking about it. But I've never touched anyone. I just can't stand to watch Sarah cry all the time. I know she's still grieving, but I need to help," William said.

57

"You need to be careful; you don't want to scare the poor girl. If she thinks you're something unpleasant, she might try and banish you. You hear about that happening more and more. The living notice one of us and assume we're nasty. Have either of you met Simon from the old pig farm, out the other side of town? He was practising, and getting very good, but the youngest realised he was there and found a banishment spell online!"

"I think they call it smudging. And I thought it was the local priest?" responded Nat.

"Regardless, he was banished from his own home, for the rest of his death! This girl needs to know that you are there to help, not harm."

"Any ideas how I manage that?"

"Not at the moment. Get better at the basics, and the solution should come to you. Why do you think she needs the help?"

"Her father and brother are getting on with things and seem to be doing quite well, but it's been months and she's still crying herself to sleep every night. She hasn't told anyone that she's still struggling, which means I'm the only one who knows. I have to help."

"You do have a duty of care. Get some rest, recharge, and we will keep practising, then you can try to help her."

Several weeks passed, following the same routine. The three ghosts would practise for a few days;

then William would go and check on Sarah. Nat would go and spend some time with Claire. Then they would start the cycle again.

During this time, William and Nat got better and more skilled. Nat was very accomplished at making his footsteps heard, and had touched Adam successfully. When I say "successfully", Adam had tried to swat the non-existent bug away from his face with too much vigour, resulting in him hitting himself rather hard in the face.

It was still hit or miss whether William could make his footsteps heard, but he too had mastered the art of tickling Adam. While in a drunken stupor, William had made him move a few times. And it was another drunken weekend for Adam.

"I want to make him laugh, not just giggle," said William.

"Go for it, boy, he's all yours." The master smiled, taking a step back and making a slight bow.

Both Nat and the master watched nervously as William began to tickle Adam's foot, which dangled over the edge of the bed. Adam's face slowly crept into a smile, then his foot twitched. Then he started smirking.

"Bob, stop it, that tickles!" He giggled sleepily.

William continued to tickle his foot, which moved more and more violently. Adam began to laugh and writhe on the bed. For William, the compulsion to keep tickling was too great; he started to tickle

Adam's sides, his other foot, under his chin, whatever he could reach.

"Bob, stop, I'm gonna pee!" shouted Adam, who was now wide awake and laughing breathlessly. William stopped, wiped a dry tear from his eye and raised his hands in triumph. Nat and the master hugged each other, cheering as if their football team had just won the FA Cup.

"I did it, I'm good!" William celebrated.

"I knew you could do it, lad," the master congratulated him.

"Well done, mate," said Nat, shaking William's hand warmly.

Meanwhile, Adam sat up in bed, still laughing to himself. Catching his breath, he said, "Bob, you bastard. It's good to know you're still here, but I think I wet myself!" He got out of bed and headed out of the room, a telltale damp patch down his trousers. He paused at the doorway and looked back into the empty room. "I won't forget you, Bob, but next time, do that to my sister." Then he walked off towards the bathroom, still smiling.

"Who the hell is Bob?" questioned Nat.

"That's what he calls me," said the master, smiling. "I was his imaginary friend – at least, his parents thought he had imagined me – when he was little. But now he's all grown up and doesn't have the time to play hide and seek with me. I'm glad he remembers me, though."

William and Nat stood agog at this revelation.

"You mean, they really know about you?" asked William.

"Of course – I've been here long enough. To most of them, I'm Bob the friendly ghost. I've made friends with most of the children over the years. When they get older, they stop wanting to play so much, but they still talk about me. It does have its downsides. I get blamed for everything that gets lost in the house, even the two bottles of port last Christmas. But at least they know I'm here, and I'm not going to hurt anyone."

Chapter 5

Having made such an impact on Adam, William felt buoyant. He was now more hopeful about helping Sarah with her grief. He still wasn't clear about how he could help, but it was now a possibility.

As he walked back through town, William spotted Sarah standing outside the supermarket. As he approached, she put her bags of shopping down, took out her phone and took a photo of a poster. Then she quickly picked up the bags and hurried off in the direction of home. William stopped and looked at the posters and cards in the window.

One advertised a mobility scooter for sale, and other aids for the elderly. Another invited people to a bingo night in aid of charity. The next was an advert for a mobile hairdresser. Then out of the corner of his eye he spotted a small but neatly printed poster.

Spend an evening with the Great Fundieni, spiritualist to the stars. Reconnect with those who have passed on. Only £25 entry. Thursday night only!

This must be what she had looked seen, he thought. Surely she wasn't gullible enough to go to something like that? William had planned on following Sarah home, but he couldn't get the idea of the Great Fundieni out of his head. Instead he decided to go to the meeting. He could fill everyone in on how he and Nat had been progressing in their lessons, and raise the subject of this Fundieni character.

William wasn't stupid; he knew that there were spiritualists and mediums out there who could hear the dead, but a guy with a name like Fundieni was unlikely to be the real deal. How could he be? Before William told the others about the poster, he had made up his mind. This man was a fraud. Probably very good at cold reading and making educated guesses, but that was all.

"There's a con man coming to town. He calls himself the Great Fundieni. He claims he's a spiritualist to the stars!" joked William.

"Fundieni – are you sure? Oh my God, we have to go. When is he coming?" said Felicia excitedly.

"It's a con, it has to be. Who in their right mind calls themselves Fundieni?" replied William.

"He is a con, but his wife isn't," Felicia said. "Do you still want to help Sarah? This could be your best shot at getting a message to her."

Thursday evening arrived. All of the dead waited with bated breath inside the town hall. Although the living outnumbered them, most of the excitement emanated from the dead.

William had spent the day working out what to say to the Great Fundieni's wife. Had he been able to sweat, his palms would be wet by now. Sarah sat quietly alone in a corner. Surrounding her was a seemingly endless supply of desperate people. Many carried photos of loved ones, though the younger ones seemed engrossed in their phones. Felicia noted one man who spent his time tweeting, then looking at photos of himself and his twin brother, then checking Facebook, then repeating the process.

After what seemed like a lifetime, the lights dimmed and the Great Fundieni stepped into a spotlight on the ageing stage.

"Good evening to you all. My name is the Great Fundieni, but you can call me Fundieni. I can see and hear that there are many spirits here, so let's not keep them waiting," he said in a suitably vague Eastern European accent. Rubbing his head, he began passing up and down the stage, the spotlight following him. "Is that a P or a B? A P – I'm getting a P. Is that Peter? Yes, Peter. I have a Peter here with us."

A woman stood up quickly, shouting excitedly, "Peter was my uncle!"

"Peter's telling me that other members of your family have recently passed over."

"Yes, that's right," said the woman.

"They were his sibling?"

The woman nodded.

"His brother?"

"Yes, my dad."

"Peter's saying he passed suddenly, but he is with your dad. He's telling me they are all alright, and that you don't need to worry about them. And he's gone. I'm sorry – that was so strong."

The woman was crying with relief. The rest of the audience applauded. The dead looked at each other in utter bewilderment. There was no Peter here, no one here with a name even close to Peter.

"I'm getting someone else coming through now…"

The ghosts looked at each other and, as one, started to head backstage to find Fundieni's wife.

At a desk sat a small woman. In front of her was a microphone. She sat with her eyes closed. Nat leaned round to see her face to check if she was asleep.

"I know you are here. Do you have a message for me?" she said without opening her eyes. Nat jumped and quickly moved out of the way.

One of the older men moved forward. "Can you tell Ida that I'm okay, and I'm glad she changed the curtains? I'm her husband, Frank."

"Frank says 'Ida, it's okay to change the curtains'. Anyone else?"

"That's amazing! Not exact but not bad," said Frank, smiling widely.

Felicia pushed William forward into the now cramped room. William recognised most of the dead, but there were a couple of faces he didn't know.

Taking a moment to compose himself, William said, "Tell Sarah her mum passed on peacefully, and didn't stay here with her." The lady paused, taking in what he had said.

"Sarah, your mother's passing was peaceful, and she is here with you."

"No, that's not right. Sarah's mother has moved on!" shouted William.

"You must move on," said the lady.

"No, her *mum* has moved on."

No response came from the woman.

"This is useless," shouted William, walking out of the room.

Back in the hall, William couldn't see Sarah. He hoped she had left before she had heard this miscommunication. Nat found William at the back of the hall, leaning against a wall, while the Great Fundieni continued his act.

"Well, at least we know how they do it. She's telling him everything we say – just not very accurately. Look, every time he starts rubbing his head, he's listening to an earpiece!"

"Did Sarah get your message?" asked Nat.

"I don't know. She was gone by the time I got out here. Hopefully not. Hearing that could make things worse for her. Do they realise the damage they can cause?"

"Most people here will leave here feeling better, I hope. Only a few will leave feeling worse. Maybe she left before, or maybe she just wanted to know if there was something after this life," replied Nat.

"We can but hope. Do you want to send a message?" asked William.

"No, Mum and Dad moved after my accident. Let's get out of here before they put the lights on and we get trampled," said Nat, as he pushed a comb through his hair.

The two ghosts stepped into the light of the dead night. Winter was definitely here. For the dead, the temperature had risen significantly. For the living, the wind bit at every exposed piece of skin. For the dead, the temperature was almost too warm. The dead don't feel hot and cold in the same way that we do. As the temperature rises, they feel more energised and are generally more active. They don't sweat or feel the need to remove clothing – but then, it's not as if they can die of heatstroke.

"What do you want to do?" asked Nat. "We can go mess with the drunks in the pub, or there's a film on."

"Who's in it?" William asked.

"The guy we saw last month in the superhero film – he played the baddie. This time, he plays the hero. What's his name?"

"I know who you mean, the tall bloke. Isn't this one an action thriller? Sounds like the best option," replied William.

With that the two ghosts headed off into the warm sunshine of the dead winter's night.

Chapter 6

The world the dead inhabit moves at a slow pace. It can take years to get to know someone. There is no need to tell someone everything about yourself all at once. After all, it's not like they are going anywhere or getting older. It's just how things are. Similarly, things move slowly when the dead are dealing with the living.

It had been several weeks since the Great Fundieni had visited their small town. William spent a lot of time watching Sarah to see if there was any improvement in her grief. She hadn't said anything to her father or brother. She hadn't even told them that she had gone, so William had no idea if she had received the garbled message or not. Sarah was still crying herself to sleep more often than not. Her grief was obviously still raw, even if only William could see it.

Christmas was just a few days away and the overall mood of the family was buoyant. Everyone was smiling more, even Sarah. Despite the cheerful decorations and the magic of Christmas, Sarah's mask still slipped behind closed doors.

"How can I make this year special for you both?" asked Luke.

"I don't know. Just do what you're doing. It's bound to be hard. It's the first Christmas without Mum," replied Sarah.

"Your aunt and uncle are coming. Paige has told me she will do all the cooking. She keeps quizzing me about presents and whether I've done all the cards."

"Have you? The last post goes on Tuesday."

"I think so," said Luke, wondering if that was true or not.

"Do you want me to check?"

"No, I should be okay. I just want it to be special for you."

"You can't make it special. The more you try, the more we'll miss her. Last Christmas was brilliant – you can't top that. Just let it happen. We need to find our feet," said Sarah, holding back what was truly in her heart.

"I suppose you're right. Next Christmas will be better, I promise. We will just try and get through this one as best we can."

Christmas Day finally arrived. The house was full of cheer and grief. With every tradition or ritual, there was the memory of the person who was missing. Mum always did it this way. Mum normally did this, or Mum would love this. All these thoughts and sentiments were experienced by the whole family at some point during the holiday period. It was a bitter pill to swallow, but everyone had to force it down regardless.

In the living room, the crackling fire played second fiddle to the massive Christmas tree. William stood at the back of the room, watching Sarah sitting alone. The flames illuminated the room, but her face in particular. She looked beautiful, yet so sad. Periodically she took a sip from her glass. Her father didn't mind her drinking under-age if she was sensible about it. So far, she had been very measured in her habits.

The heat of the dead winter was almost unbearable, but William enjoyed the cooling effect of the fire. He had spent most of the day with his back to the cold fire, allowing his body to regulate rather than cook.

A heavy snow had fallen a few days earlier. For the living, staying warm when the weather was cold was key. For the dead, the snow has a cooling effect, offering some relief from the boiling summer temperatures the dead feel when they went outside. William used this dead air con as an excuse to follow Sarah's family, and Sarah in particular. When no one was around, she was able to relax and let her act drop. Maintaining it must be exhausting, but she played the part well, and maybe if she faked it long enough, she would make it real, William thought.

It was getting late. Sarah was the last one up after such a long day. Having finished her drink, she made her way to bed. William checked that the others were asleep while Sarah got ready for bed. Then he watched as she drifted off to sleep, without crying this time.

"Soon it will be a new year. You'll be able to start over. We all will," he said quietly, as he left the room and hurried off into the heat of the dead day.

Down at the mill, all the dead had gathered. With a thick layer of snow all around them, it was very festive. For the dead it was far from cold; it felt more like a summer party. The dead day was spent singing Christmas songs, telling stories and laughing. The master tried to instigate a snowball fight, but it's not the same when each snowball flies through its intended victim. Nevertheless, they all had fun trying to throw snow at each other.

In a nearby tree, mistletoe grew from every bough. Nat and Claire shared a passionate kiss under it, and everyone cheered. All of them laughed when one of the butchers forced a kiss onto the lips of the other. At any other time, this would have resulted in the two of them fighting, but it was

Christmas, so they smiled and hugged each other as only family can.

It was a magical time, and the best Christmas William had spent since he died. Everyone was happy, talking, joking and dancing in the snow. For all those who gathered at the mill, the dead day had gone too fast. With the dawn of the new day, the living began Boxing Day, which they spent nursing a hangover induced by food or alcohol, or both. In the meantime, the dead started telling stories. Then as the living slept through *The Great Escape*, their stories became more ghostly – obviously told from the ghost's perspective.

The group had slowly moved from the mill to the stream as the light dwindled. They were all happy and relaxed, exuberant and exhausted by the day.

"Have any of you heard the story of Pa?" asked William from his reclining position.

"Yes," said Felicia, raising her hand in agreement.

"No? That's perfect," replied William, leaning forward to better see the group. "Then I'll begin."

Chapter 7

Pa was, at best, average when he was alive. He had tried his hand at several jobs, but the only thing he excelled at was Christmas. Not just for his own children, but for others.

At an early age he had gone grey-haired, then quickly white. With that came a well-formed gut. "Cuddly" would be the polite way of describing him. But he used his physical appearance to his advantage.

He not only dressed as Santa Claus for his children, but also for the children at the local shopping centre. Year after year he brought joy to many a child. He enjoyed the simple joy of making others happy. He might have had a strong local accent, but the tone and intent in his voice were hypnotic to children.

Some commented on the marks or the colour of his nose. His response: "Frostbite. Spent too long over Canada a few years back." The country varied, yet the implication of his bravery was always there, not the reality (summers spent consuming too much cider).

To the children, he was Santa. He became such a regular that he even had his own handmade suit. Not the shop-bought version such as an amateur would use – no. Pa was a professional. He regrew his beard for every Christmas. Should a rogue hair dare come through as anything but white, the bathroom bleach would fix that.

For Pa, the role he played for two weeks of the year made the rest of the year bearable. Seeing so many happy children made him happy. It also gave him a valid excuse to leave all the Christmas preparations to his loving wife.

When his own children had been very small, he had worked so hard to make ends meet that he had missed out on their childhoods. Food and rent had been a higher priority than play or time. Then when they were slightly older, work paid better, and his true persona had been born. They had cottoned on quickly to his disguise but played along anyway, perhaps believing that this would get them bigger or better presents.

All too soon, his children had grown up, and he was left playing Santa to others only. But he never stopped, secretly knowing that one day there would be grandchildren who, like their parents, would be mesmerised by the arrival of Santa in their own home.

The last year had been a step too far for Pa. He had done the shopping centre, two schools and the children's ward in quick succession. His grand entrance – through an obliging window, as there wasn't a chimney – was his last. Halfway through, he felt his chest tighten and his vision blur. A massive heart attack killed Pa – and his grandchildren's belief in Santa. They had witnessed too much. At first they were excited at his visit at this midnight hour, then confused as he was lifted into an ambulance, his face covered against the blinding, flashing blue light.

Pa was buried in his beloved Santa suit. He loved it, and after the night of horror, no one wanted it. He had mastered his trade before. Now that he was dead and stuck, he would learn it afresh. He carried on in a similar fashion as before. Only now he appeared as if by magic, then disappeared on cue to those children who were most in need of faith and magic at this time of year. He started with his grandchildren. The look of relief and wonder on their faces made his lies count as truth.

"I know that I died, and I'm sorry that you had to see that. But I have got the job of actually being Santa Claus. You will be fine without me, and I will see you every Christmas Eve – if you believe in me. I love you all. And I always will," he said, before disappearing before their eyes.

He lingered for a few weeks after that encounter, comforted by the way the children spoke of Pa, visiting them and telling them how he was now the real Santa. His own children took this as a sign of grief, but at least they were happy and no longer miserable at the thought of Christmas.

Then came the miners' strike. Pa had visited several places, taking his time, talking to different children, asking them what they really wanted, perched on the end of their beds. Then he insisted: "You had better write it down for me. I've forgotten my notepad, and me memory isn't as good as it should be. Your parents will be able to send it for you" – in the hope that savvy parents would be able to check and find out what their child really wanted. He would do this for several children in the build-up to Christmas. But a visit from him on Christmas Eve was always reserved for those in most need.

That fateful night, Pa had chosen a modest house that had seen its fair share of misfortune that year. The elderly grandmother had passed away, and more and more beloved items had to be sold off to pay for food or rent. The miners' strike hit hardest as Christmas approached. For this family, it would be bleak indeed.

Pa stood and looked at where the Christmas tree should have been. Instead, a healthy pot plant played a good stand-in. It was green, just not sturdy enough to withstand many baubles. The old lights had caused slight brown patches to form on its leaves, but they were easily covered with tinsel.

Underneath were three small packages. All were wrapped carefully in newspaper and finished with a bow. Pa knelt to read the names aloud, so the children could hear. "This one's for Sam, this one is for David. And because I think she deserves it, a little something for Mum."

Pa was not only heard, but was also visible to the living. He turned around to see the joy and wonder on the children's faces, but was greeted by the father. He was halfway down the stairs and approaching fast.

"How dare you steal from us – and in that suit?" he shouted as he launched himself at Pa. His fists were raised, ready to get in the first blow. His wife and two children huddled together at the top of the stairs, fear etched on their faces. Their expressions quickly changed as their father passed silently and effortlessly through Pa and into the Christmas plant. Baubles rolled all over the place, and tinsel and hot lights tangled themselves around the father, pinning him in place.

Pa picked up a bauble and turned to face the angry man. "You never really believed in me, did you? That's why I never got you the bike you asked for. Maybe next year you'll do better and get off the naughty list!" he said, handing him the bauble.

The remaining family members had joined them near the bottom of the stairs. "I'm sorry, you two," said Pa, kneeling to meet their gaze. "You have both been so good this year. But I'm afraid we have a strike of our own to deal with." Looking at the mother, he said, "The elves are striking." He turned back to the two children. "We have all had to tighten our belts this year." Unconsciously, he patted his belly as he stood.

"That's okay, Santa. If I got an expensive present. my friends might get upset. Will next year be better?" asked the eldest child.

"Of course. There is only one way to go when you hit rock bottom, and that's up. Slowly but surely, things will get better," Pa replied reassuringly.

Pa then took the mother's hand and kissed it gently. "My complements – your house is a credit to you. May I wish you a happy Christmas and a wonderful new year!"

"And the same to you and your family," replied the woman, sounding scared yet with the hint of a smile.

With a wink to the children, he shouted, "Ho, ho, ho" as he slowly melted from view.

"He can't be real? He was never real. But how did he know about the bike?" asked the father as he finally got free of the plant. "But he was here in our house..."

"We told you he was real, Daddy!" shouted the younger child, darting past his father to check that he hadn't damaged the valuable presents. The mother just stood there in shock.

"Why did I stop believing?" she muttered, slowly sinking to sit on the bottom stair. "Or have we all gone mad?"

Pa left the children happy and looking forward to Christmas the following day, their faith concreted into their minds. By contrast, the parents didn't know what to think about what had happened, or how to react to it. Regardless, their lives had been changed – and would stay that way forever.

That night, Pa went from being just another ghost in a weird outfit to the legend that will forever be Pa.

Chapter 8

New Year's Eve went off just as Christmas Day had. Felicia, Mark, Claire, Nat and William had decided they would go out clubbing. William wasn't surprised to find out that Mark enjoyed clubbing. What did surprise him was that Stan, an older male ghost, also seemed to relish the idea.

Nightclubs are great for the dead. You might think that's because they're dark inside, but that's not the reason. Seeing so many living people enjoying themselves is intoxicating for the dead. Ghosts can join in the dancing and singing, but they also get a massive high. As William had discovered before, among so many people, if somehow you are seen, the living assume that you're just one of them. Their odd clothes, William presumed, were seen as fancy dress.

They all walked in past the line of people patiently waiting outside. In the club the bass was already loud, the lights flashed and traced across the room. The dance floor was full of people partying. Most of the crowd were dressed in their best pulling outfits. Some had New Year hats on, but not all. The men mostly wore trousers and shirts, whereas the women wore short, clingy or revealing dresses.

The noise was immense and soon everyone, even the ghosts, had to shout to be heard. Felicia made a beeline to some tables and placed the bouncing baby Mark on one of them. Having kissed him on his forehead, she left him to party on his own and joined the others on the dance floor.

"What have you done with Mark?" asked William.

"He's over there," responded Felicia, pointing in his general direction. "It's what he likes."

From a distance William could see he was happy and getting down to the beat in his own unique way. It was obvious why she had put him on a table. He really seemed to get into the music, and on the table, he could throw himself around. Unable to knock the glasses over and without being stood on by the living, he could enjoy himself on his own dance floor.

The group of ghosts spent the night hovering around the dance floor. They would join in whenever they felt the rhythm take them, just as the living did. In a short time, they were all drunk on the waves of energy coming off the living. Whenever a slower song came on, Felicia would fetch Mark and the two would dance quietly as only good friends could. They was no hint of sex between them, just pure platonic love. William admired this greatly, as would anyone who witnessed them, as they embraced and slowly swayed to the groove.

William danced with everyone that night, and even had a few slow dances with Felicia and Claire. He soaked up the atmosphere with enthusiasm. Then came the countdown. The dead screamed as loudly as the living, their voices lost in the melee of so many. "Ten, nine, eight, seven, six, five, four, three, two, one – happy new year!" Then, as is the tradition, everyone in the club, both living and dead, joined hands to sing 'Old Lang Syne'.

William kissed all of the ghosts on the lips and hugged everyone as they celebrated. We're not talking about the sort of passionate kiss that Nat and Claire shared, but the friendly peck on the lips that you might get from a relative or a good friend. They had shared nothing in life, but now they were dead, they were all family.

The night continued with lots of dancing, laughter and soaking up the energy of the living. At the end of the night, the lights came on full. The ghosts congregated near the stage, where the only sounds were those of the staff cleaning up.

"We need to do this more often," said Nat.

"Yes, definitely. If only to see old Stan here twerk!" William giggled.

"I haven't been to anything like this for years. Dodgy hip. An advantage to being dead is that all the aches and pains are gone," said Stan.

"Shall we say every Friday?" asked William.

"Yes!" replied Claire. "We all need this on a regular basis. Was it me, or did it feel like a huge thunderstorm?"

Everyone agreed. Every Friday night they would frequent the town's nightclub, giving themselves a healthy boost. However, next time they would try and convince the others to come. Nat and William were determined to see what the master would do on the dance floor. Or would he spend the night playing tricks on the drunken stag and hen parties?

William returned to the house, buoyant after his night out. The new year had arrived, yet there was no visible change. The streets he passed down remained the same as before. The living were few and far between. The faces of the people he passed showed something that was observable: hope. Hope that their lot in life would improve in the months to come. Hope that resolutions made last night and begun today would change things dramatically.

Even though the sun was high, there was little evidence of it through the thick cloud. For William and the others, this meant they could make their way around by the dim moonlight of the dead night. Had any of the dead accidentally knocked something over, no one living would have noticed. The living, unlike the dead, were having to recover from the exploits of the night before. The dead, by contrast, were full of energy, and keen to use it.

William walked through the locked front door. Inside, there was the odd glass left unwashed, telling him that last night had been, in the most part, positive for the family. Upstairs they were all still asleep. He ventured from room to room, trying to unravel the events and experiences of the hours before they had gone to bed. All that he could see pointed to a pleasant and relatively joyous night.

This emotional equilibrium continued for the next few days. Then William saw Sarah ripping pieces of paper into neat squares. His gut twisted and fear engulfed him.

Chapter 9

In her room, Sarah carefully tore a sheet of paper into small pieces. Then she wrote a different letter of the alphabet on each piece, then the numbers 0 to 9. Finally she wrote the words "yes", "no", "hello" and "goodbye" on the remaining squares.

William knew what would happen next. If he could have turned pale with panic, he would have. For she was making her own Ouija board.

"Snap out of this! Sarah, if you can hear me, don't do this. You can't be stupid enough to try this. Please don't do this," he pleaded.

But his begging went unheard. He tried moving the pen away. But the tiny movement went unnoticed by Sarah. He stamped his feet, pleading for her to stop, but she could not hear him. He blew at the pile of ripped paper, but the best he could muster was a slight flutter of the top piece. Sarah did notice this. Her response was to shut the curtains and make sure the door was firmly closed.

The more desperate William got, the less effect his actions had. William began to panic, and his stomach rolled with anticipation. Sarah became more excited and focused on the task in hand. She wanted to talk to her mother once more.

It was Friday night. Nat and Claire had planned to visit William, then go on together to the club. As they walked along hand in hand, they felt something unusual. It was a sort of tingling throughout their bodies, a bit like pins and needles, but this was everywhere, not just in their extremities. Turning into William's street, they could see why.

William's house glowed with a vibrant green light. They ran towards it, anxious. As they got closer, the tingling got worse.

"What is that light?" asked Claire.

"I don't know, but it doesn't feel good," said Nat, sounding very concerned.

"William is gonna need help, whatever that is," said Claire.

"Oh God. What's happening?" shouted Claire as they passed through the front door. The house was shaking with a deafening, never-ending rumble.

Nat shook his head. "We need to find William! This is bad, very bad."

From upstairs they dimly heard William shouting. Through the din they couldn't make out what he was yelling, just that it was him. The two followed his voice upstairs as fast as they could. They entered Sarah's room, to see a scene of chaos. Everything was shaking violently. William stood next to Sarah, shouting at her.

"Stop! You have to stop. Please, your mother's gone. Stop this!" shouted William. He turned as Nat and Claire entered. Next to them, a blank space on the wall began rippling, like tiny waves on water.

They all backed away instinctively.

"She's doing a Ouija board. It's opening a doorway. I can't make her stop. You have to help me!" William shouted, as they all stared at what had been a wall.

Claire went straight to Sarah and tried shouting herself. "Stop! You have to stop before it's too late!"

But Sarah heard nothing. Only the dead could fully experience what was happening. The wall began to slowly morph into something door-shaped. The two men stood in front of it, fists clenched, ready to fight whatever came out.

Claire moved round to face Sarah. She placed one hand on the glass on the table in front of her, and the other on her head. Closing her eyes to concentrate, she began muttering to herself. Behind her, the door was fully formed. William and Nat glanced at each other, then rushed at it. The door was opening.

Claire focused her mind. "Stop. Danger. Stop. Danger." She repeated it over and over again under her breath. Under her hand, the glass began to move.

"O," said Sarah, writing it down on her notepad. "P. D. A. N." She said the letters one by one as the glass moved slowly back and forth. Unaware of the chaos that the dead were experiencing, she remained calm. The door had opened an inch or so. William and Nat tried with all their strength to shut it.

"G. E. R. S." Sarah and Claire were both totally focused. Claire continued to mutter to herself, while Sarah patiently watched the glass move from one letter to the next. "T. O. P."

William and Nat wedged themselves against the door, but it continued to open slowly. A long, thin, mutilated hand reached round its edge. It gripped the door. Its flesh burned into the wood. Its nails dug in, narrowly missing William's arm, but ripping the fabric of his shirt.

"Danger. Stop. Danger. Stop." Claire's chant continued, unheard over the cacophony of noise. Sarah looked at the notepad. Fear gripped her as she read the message.

OPDANGERSTOP

Without thinking, she let go of the glass. At the same second, the door slammed shut; the hand and its owner vanished. The house fell silent and still once more. Claire opened her eyes and let go of

Sarah's head and the glass. Sarah leaned forward and forced the glass to "Goodbye", then collapsed back into her chair.

"You did it. You're amazing!" said William, as he and Nat peeled themselves off the floor and away from the door.

"I know. Why do you think I fell for her?" replied Nat as he dusted himself down. Claire rushed to embrace him. Nat held her close and kissed her. The door behind them remained, but it was closed. "You were bloody lucky, mate," Nat said, looking at William.

"You're telling me," William replied as he embraced Nat and Claire. Relief filled the three ghosts. But the door remained.

Sarah pulled herself forward and looked at the notepad once more. *OPDANGERSTOP* stared at her from the page. She crossed out the first two letters to reveal the true message: *DANGERSTOP*. The message was clear and terrifying.

The ghosts watched as Sarah picked up all the pieces of paper and the glass and put them in the bin, then took the bin outside. In the garden, Sarah opened the garden incinerator. Working by torchlight, she emptied the contents of the bin into it. Old bits of newspaper and dried-up plants were already inside. She calmly took out a lighter and set light to it all.

All four of them watched as the flames took hold. The glass at first blackened then smashed gently against the rest of the burning waste.

With the immediate danger over, the three ghosts watched in silence as Sarah returned to her room, climbed into bed and fell into a deep sleep. But the door remained. The three then began to stagger back towards the mill. Exhausted, they said nothing to each other but just focused on the task of walking.

In the bright light of the dead night the mill stood like a beacon of safety among the bare fields and empty sky. Having crossed the threshold, all three ghosts collapsed into unconsciousness. Others had gathered for tonight's outing to the club, but since they had no explanation for what had just happened, fear spread through them. Being out for the count was a very rare thing for a ghost. The others knew something had to be done. So the two butchers ran to fetch the master – the only person who might know what to do.

Chapter 10

Morning light flowed gently through the curtains. As it hit Sarah's eyes, she slowly woke from a fitful sleep. The night before had been terrifying, yet exhilarating. She pulled herself out of bed, washed, and dressed as normal. The sounds of her brother and father waking and doing the same signalled the start of the day.

Sarah sat at her dressing table, slowly applying make-up then sorting out her hair. Her mind was still struggling with what had happened the previous night. *She had made contact.* That was the main thought inside her head. But why did her mother want her to stop? And why was it so dangerous? These thoughts rattled round her head, holding her attention.

School would begin again the next day. She had to focus on her coursework and prepare for her exams, even though they were months ahead. Sarah knew how important they were. She had to focus. But the questions in her mind had nothing to do with Shakespeare's influence on modern popular culture, or the best way to solve algebraic equations. They were far more fundamental. She needed to understand more.

In that moment, she was hooked. The world of the paranormal had pulled her in and trapped her. Her studies didn't have the same addictive quality.

Over breakfast, she was in a world of her own, replaying the events of last night over and over again in her head.

"You alright? Not woken up yet?" asked her dad.

"Didn't sleep well. Probably just thinking about this term too much," she replied.

"You were up late. I heard you moving around after two," interrupted Oliver in between mouthfuls of cereal.

"What were you doing awake at that time?" asked Luke.

"I-I couldn't sleep. I stayed up to watch a film. But it is the holidays!" protested Oliver.

"That was the last time. You're back at school tomorrow. If I catch you doing that during term-time, I'll have to take your TV. I've warned you before. Third time's the charm," Luke said sternly.

Sarah's attention had drifted back to more important things. Last night, her hand had been on the glass, but she hadn't moved it. She stared into her cereal bowl. Had she been paying more attention, she would have realised she was in bed asleep well before 2 a.m.

"You both need an early night tonight. That means no TV after nine – and yes, I am talking to you," said Luke, pointing at Oliver.

His looked down into his bowl. He was in trouble, and he knew it. He smiled to himself, realising that there was nothing he particularly wanted to see until Thursday night. By then his dad would have calmed down, forgotten or just given up. He would be fine.

Sarah remained rapt in thought, but continued to do what was required throughout the day. Whatever had happened, she needed to know more. The big question was, how? If talking to her mother through the Ouija board was dangerous, then she would have to find another method.

Back in the world of the dead, there was pandemonium at the mill. With the dead night approaching fast, the butchers Ethan and Tom ran to the manor to find the master. He was by far the oldest, and therefore the most likely to know what to do.

"Did anyone hear them say anything?" asked Stan.

"No," replied a chorus of confused ghosts.

"Let's move them into the mill and try and make them comfortable at least," Felicia suggested to the group.

One by one the unconscious ghosts were carefully carried into the mill. Regardless of whether or not you were living or dead, anyone watching would have had a knot in the pit of their stomach. Not because of the bodies laid out among the rubble, but because of the unnatural silence. The worry and fear coming off those standing guard wasn't just palpable; it was a living entity with teeth and claws. It stalked everyone present, spying on them from every vantage point, waiting to strike with deadly force. A rabbit not too far away sensed this danger, turned tail and ran. The subtle noise was enough to make everyone flinch.

Hours seemed to pass before the master appeared – a reassuring sight to the worried ghosts. The two butchers were as good as their word. Despite the dark, they had run as fast as they could to the manor house.

"You have to come quickly. Something really bad has happened to Nat, Claire and William," gasped Ethan.

"They're all unconscious at the mill," said Tom, his chest heaving after the run.

"What happened? Ghosts don't just pass out," questioned the master, sounding concerned.

"We don't know. We had planned to go to the club later," answered Tom.

"When we were all about to leave, they turned up at the mill and just dropped," said Ethan breathlessly.

"They didn't say anything – they just looked wrecked."

"We ran here to get you. You have to come quickly."

"We have to go now!" the butchers said in tandem. Finishing each other's sentences wasn't uncommon between these two. But the panic on their faces was unheard of. The master recognised this and quickly followed them out of the house. Despite the darkness, they took a shortcut through a small wood. Quickly they were out of it and running through open fields. Their pace quickened.

"What happened? Tell me everything!" shouted the master when he reached the mill.

"We don't know. They arrived looking awful, then they collapsed," said Stan.

"We brought them in here – they passed out over there," said Felicia, pointing vaguely into the darkness. The butchers had now caught up with the master. Patting each other on the back, they stood bowed and breathing heavily. Had they had a pulse, they would have been floored by this workout.

"Any change?" panted Ethan.

"No," replied Felicia as she nervously chewed her fingers.

The master dropped to his knees and examined each victim in turn, first looking into their eyes. In the darkness there was nothing to see, not even the merest spark of life. He then placed his hand on their head, then their chest.

"We have to get them to the water, now! Quickly, or we might lose them," ordered the master.

The ghosts did not respond verbally, but rapidly grabbed the unconscious spirits and dragged them as fast as they could to the stream.

"Don't worry about being careful. If they survive, they won't mind being manhandled," said the master. Felicia and Tom were already out of the doorway, dragging Claire by her legs.

"When you get them there, make sure they are in contact with the water," the master called.

In no time, all three victims were lying beside the stream, with either a hand or foot in the water. This was an unusual request from the master, but no one questioned his wisdom. If a ghost placed a hand in a water source for any more than few seconds, they would get a shock similar to that of static: the power of the shock would be dictated by the power of the water source. A stream untamed like this one was only slightly weaker than a large river. Despite this, the three remained totally lifeless.

"Good. We will have to swap them round regularly. But we have to find out what happened to them," said the master as he viewed the scene before him. "Whatever did happen, it will have to wait until we can see clearly. You lads rest up, you've done a lot tonight, but I will need your help tomorrow." The master looked at the two exhausted butchers lying in the grass. A simple thumbs up from them both acknowledged the request.

Throughout the rest of the dark day, the three were closely monitored. Whenever their extremity started to blacken, it was removed from the water and replaced with another. Felicia and the master mingled with the group without saying much. Simply placing a hand on someone's shoulder, then smiling reassuringly at them, was enough. For all of those present, this was by far the longest night of their deaths.

"What caused this?" Felicia asked again.

"I don't know. I've only heard of ghosts going through this. But I never knew the cause. I do know it's not burnout," answered the master.

"They wouldn't burn out, they're not that type."

"I know, but whatever did this is dangerous, so we all have to be on our guard," replied the master. "Just keep turning them; we'll know more when they wake."

"Don't you mean *if* they wake" said Ethan, concerned.

"Don't be defeatist, boy, there is still hope. And we can see what's what in the morning. Do we know where they were?" asked the master.

"I think Nat and Claire were going to William's house, then on to the club," answered Stan. "We were all about to leave ourselves when they came in and dropped to the floor."

"And you're sure they didn't say anything?" asked the master.

"No. Nat got closest to me and the mill. He looked right through me and Mark, then his eyes rolled back into his head and he hit the floor," said Felicia, gently stroking Claire's forehead.

No one had the courage to ask the obvious, but they were all thinking the same. *Could this happen to me?* That monster that stalked their minds was growing. How long until they all succumbed to it? After all, death and disease were not beyond anyone, not even those already dead.

For ghosts, addiction to negative energies spread like a virus. Once a ghost was infected, it was almost impossible to recover. Once the infection took hold, it always led to burnout. A vile and painful way to die. The victim would literally burn up, leaving nothing but ash. And all ghosts of a reasonable age would have witnessed this at some point.

It used to be that the threat of being sent to Bedlam Mental Hospital could prevent a further descent into madness. The same could be said for burnout. Now, knowing how it could end would scare most souls away from the negative energies given off by the living. This fear would prevent most from causing harm, but not all.

Chapter 11

After what seemed like an age, the dawn of a new dead day came. The three victims remained in the same state. While the living wound down and eventually slept, the dead roamed. Charged by the warmth of the dead winter, they were able to do more and for longer.

They decided that Felicia and the others would monitor the three comatose ghosts, turning them when needed. Meanwhile the master and the two butchers, Ethan and Tom, would go out to find out what could have caused this.

First they checked the nightclub, attempting to retrace the steps taken by the three, but there was nothing obvious there. They moved quietly and with caution through the busy club, checking first the main floor then the bar. Despite the hustle and bustle of the living setting up around them, they became increasingly nervous as they checked the toilets, back rooms and offices. But there was nothing that appeared out of place.

"There's nothing here. It either happened to them on the way here or at William's house," remarked Tom.

"We should retrace their route here," replied the master.

"There's only one place we haven't checked here: the cellar," said Ethan.

"I didn't know there was a cellar," said the master.

"This used to be the White Stag pub. They kept the barrels downstairs."

"And how do you know that?" asked Tom.

"I stepped out with the barmaid a few times!" Ethan said, smiling to himself. "She had an amazing chest," he continued, his thoughts drifting back to this youthful conquest. "It's this way," he said, snapping himself out it.

Down in the cellar they found nothing but darkness and booze. Barrels for the pumps upstairs, crates of drinks seemingly in every colour you could want, and one fat rat eating his weight in salted peanuts.

"There's nothing here. We had better move on. We've still got a lot of ground to cover," said the master, gently kicking a barrel of beer.

The three ghosts walked through the town's almost empty streets. With the shops closed, there were few pedestrians out. Only taxis passed them, carrying revellers to and from their previous night destinations. The butchers took one side of the high street each, walking in and out of the shuttered shops, looking for clues. The master stayed outside, walking down the centre of the road so he could survey the whole picture.

"Anything?" he asked Ethan.

"Yes, the bakery has bought a new doughnut machine. It's all shiny and new. But nothing else," he replied.

"Anything your side?" the master asked Tom.

"Just "closing down" signs in the clothes shop."

"Well, that's the town searched. Just the houses between here and William's to check," said the master.

"Do we need to check them all?" asked Tom.

"No, just keep your eyes open on the way. I think that's where we will find what did this," replied the master.

The three spirits were several streets away when they came across the cat. He was sitting on a garden wall, apparently waiting for them. He jumped down to greet them as they approached.

"Isn't that the cat from William's place?" asked Ethan as he bent down to stroke him.

"I think so. What are you doing here? What's wrong with your place, I wonder," said the master as the cat wound around his legs. "I think we have our first clue."

When they rounded the corner into William's road, they could all feel it. Slight pins and needles in their hands and feet. The master said nothing, but walked on with more purpose. He recognised the feeling and knew what it could mean.

As they approached the front door he said, "We're looking for a door that shouldn't be there. If it's open, then we are all in trouble. Don't open it. Be on your guard, boys. If you get into trouble, yell and get out quick. We'll meet up there." He pointed to the end of the street. The two butchers looked at each other. They had both been uneasy before this statement, but now their unease had developed into absolute fear.

Ethan and Tom stayed close to each other as they moved from room to room downstairs. They met the master at the bottom of the stairs. Nothing was said, just a knowing nod exchanged. Then they ascended the stairs.

They all peered into the spare room. Nothing unusual there. Then Oliver's room. Nothing but a boy lying flat out in the bed. Light from the dead day was fading fast, so all the living were safely tucked up in bed.

The master looked into Sarah's room. He stopped for a few seconds, his head inside and the bulk of his body outside. Then he marched in. A moment later, his arm appeared. With a finger he beckoned them inside.

In the room, the three all stood and stared at the new door. "Found it!" said the master.

"What is that?" asked Tom nervously.

"That is a portal," replied the master. He bent down to get a closer look.

"Don't touch it!" exclaimed Ethan.

"Don't worry, I wasn't. But here, look – scratch marks," said the master, pointing to the frame. "I think something tried to come through. That must be what did for our friends. They stopped it somehow."

"What do we do about it? We can't just leave it here," asked Ethan.

"We can't get rid of it; only the living can do that. But it's still very dangerous. We need to guard it, make sure no one opens it. Whatever tried to get through will be waiting on the other side for a chance. Ethan, will you take first watch with me?"

"Um, yes. So long as I don't have to be here on my own," he responded nervously.

"Good. And no, no one should be here alone. Tom, you go back to the mill. Fill the others in and try and sort a rota system for guarding this thing. We need to keep an eye on this round the clock, and monitor the others. It might be a while before they come around."

Ethan and Tom nodded in agreement.

Chapter 12

7 a.m. Sarah's alarm went off. The master and Ethan jumped. They had spent most of the night sitting on the floor in silence at the foot of her bed, watching the door. Sarah got up. It was the first day back at school. She showered, dried her hair, then put on her uniform, unaware of the door of the two ghosts standing out in the hall. Once she had left the room, Ethan followed her downstairs, while the master re-entered the bedroom.

Just as the living were leaving the house to start their day, Felicia and Stan arrived. They had come to change shifts with Ethan and the master.

"Are you both okay?" asked Felicia as she dodged Luke in the hallway.

"Yes, just tired. How are things back at the mill?" replied Ethan.

"No change yet. Where's the master?"

"Upstairs. I'll show you up." Ethan led the way to Sarah's bedroom. The master was sitting on the end of the bed, still watching the door.

"Evening. How did last night go?" asked Stan as he shook the master's hand firmly.

"Nothing happened. Long may that remain. But this is the door," said the master. All four of them stood for a moment and stared at it, willing it to disappear, but fearful of what lay behind it.

"We can't get rid of it, can we?" questioned Felicia.

"No, only the living can remove something that's been summoned by the living."

"So, we have to get Sarah to undo what she did. Well, we're assuming she did it," said the master.

"How?" asked Stan.

"Smudging, or get a priest in to get rid of it," said Ethan.

"The important question is, how do we tell her to do this? The living can't even see the bloody thing, and let's face it, William's been trying for ages to get a message to her," replied Felicia.

"Yes, and we can't scare her. This thing is giving off enough bad vibes as it is. We will all have to try and get the message across, carefully," said the master.

"It will give us something to do while we're watching this thing," replied Stan, shivering at the thought of it.

After the living had gone out, the house fell silent. Felicia and Stan assumed the position, sitting on the end of Sarah's bed, waiting for something to happen.

It was getting dark when Sarah and Oliver returned home. It had been a long day for them both. Before they changed out of their uniforms, they went to the kitchen, where they sat eating biscuits out of the tin with a cup of hot tea.

"So, what happened with that little twat?" asked Sarah.

"Nothing," replied Oliver.

"Nothing, really? You can talk to me, you know. I can help."

"He didn't say anything today."

"But…"

"But he shoved me."

"Did anyone see? Did you tell?"

"No. And the last time he was called into the office, it got worse. It's not just him, but his mates. It's better if I keep my mouth shut." Oliver hunted for another chocolate biscuit.

"He will stop, eventually," replied Sarah reassuringly. "I'm sorry you have to put up with him. I love you." She gave him a hug and a kiss on the forehead. She wanted so badly to tell him that their mother was still around, and that everything was going to be okay. But she couldn't. How could she tell him that she had made contact? She didn't understand it herself. Oliver would never admit it, but he was still having nightmares, which was understandable. He had witnessed his mother's slow and painful death, up close and in vivid Technicolor. He didn't need to worry about how his mother might be watching them. Their mother was obviously scared of something. But was she still suffering in death as she had in her last days of life?

Sarah's thoughts once more bounced from the day-to-day to the world of the paranormal. She had to find out more. She needed to talk to her mother, but she had to find another way to do that. The Ouija board had worked, but if it was dangerous, she couldn't risk it again. Sarah, like most, had seen her fair share of horror films. Her family had been through enough without then welcoming something nasty into their lives.

During lunchtime, she had gone to the library. Rather than sitting on the internet, she had searched the shelves for anything that might help. But the books there were all ghost stories; they weren't real. They offered no advice for how to contact the dead. All they seemed to focus on were times when a bad spirit had come into someone's life and pushed them to the point of insanity. She had been warned, so she would tread carefully, and that meant research.

That evening Sarah sat on her bed, cross-legged, waiting for her computer to warm up. Then she went straight to the internet. *Contacting the dead*, she typed. Felicia and Stan stood at either side of the bed, craning to get a look at what she was doing. 756,000,000 results. She would have to narrow down her search. *Ways to contact the dead*, she typed and hit search. 337,560,000 results. That was still too many, but she scrolled down anyway. Near the top of the page were adverts from people claiming to be able to speak to a lost loved one for you. Then halfway down came a selection of clips from YouTube.

Out of the five clips shown, three involved the hit show *Mostly Ghostly*. By this point, Felicia and Stan were so close they were almost touching her, but she remained unaware. She clicked on the first link and up popped a clip. It was forty-five minutes long – a full episode. Sarah settled back against her pillows as the credits rolled.

"Tonight, on *Mostly Ghostly* we are investigating the Old Pump Rooms here in historic Bristol," the presenter said brightly.

Sarah was already engrossed. They weren't just visiting, they were actively investigating somewhere. Here, at last, she might get some useful advice.

Sarah, Felicia and Stan watched the entire episode. The ghosts knelt by the bed to see the screen and to be a bit more comfortable. There wasn't enough room on the single bed for anyone but Sarah to sit. When the first clip ended, another automatically started. The three of them were mesmerised.

"This is amazing. Do you think those machines actually work?" asked Stan.

"I don't know. The master might know. If only she could get hold of one, we could tell her everything!" replied Felicia.

"Morning!" beamed two older gentlemen as they entered the room.

"We're here to take over from you," said George.

"Anything of interest?" asked John.

"She's watching *Mostly Ghostly*; they're amazing. Nuts, but amazing. I wouldn't go there if you paid me," replied Stan.

"Hopefully, we can get some useful ideas from it, as well as Sarah," said Felicia. "Thankfully, no change with the door." She pointed to it. "How are the others?"

"No change yet. The master says it could be a while. I guess time will tell," responded George.

"I want to keep watching, but we had better get back. Any thoughts as to how you can communicate with her?" Felicia asked.

"Neither of us can do anything, so the master told just to keep an eye on things for now," replied John.

"You get back and get some rest. I'm sure we'll all still be here at the next change of shift," said George. With that, Felicia and Stan walked out of the room and back to the sanctuary of the mill.

Chapter 13

The next few weeks passed quickly. The ghosts took turns in looking after the victims, who still lay lifeless by the stream, and guarding the door. The older and more experienced ghosts tried all they could to communicate with Sarah. Just a single word – "smudge" or "smudging". Although it's a simple word, its ramifications were huge. "Smudging" was the only way to get rid of the door. But this was something that only the living could do, as it was the living who had summoned the door in the first place.

Unfortunately for the ghosts, all attempts had fallen on deaf ears. From Sarah's perspective, nothing had happened since she'd tried the Ouija board. She had instead been engrossed in research and school. She had watched hours of *Mostly Ghostly* and had got some good ideas. Sadly, the most reliable methods they used were out of her price range. Buying a voice recorder and night vision cameras was too much. What she needed was something low-tech but effective.

Sarah was sitting on the floor, sorting through piles of papers. Her coursework was due in the next few days, and she had let things slide. Tom, Felicia and Mark entered, walked round her and sat on the bed.

"Are you sure you want Mark near this thing?" asked Tom.

"He'll be fine; he hasn't left the mill in weeks. And that damn thing hasn't done anything. It just sits there looking at you," Felicia replied, as she put Mark on the floor to crawl around and wander.

"Where's that gone? Umm. It was here a minute ago," said Sarah as she rifled through a pile of papers to her left. "It's got a great big graph on the front. How can I not see it?"

"It's here, dear," said Tom, as he looked at all the pieces of paper strewn across the bed.

"Ah ha! Found you," replied Sarah, picking it up, oblivious to the ghost trying to help. Tom and Felicia watched the piles slowly build up into five distinct stacks. Meanwhile Mark was crawling all over the place, but not near the door. He pulled himself up onto the chair. Felicia saw his attempts to climb and put him on the dresser. Now, up where he wanted to be, he smiled as he looked around him. Felicia left him to it, and rejoined Tom on the bed.

"When did she say all this needed to be done by?" asked Felicia.

"The biology has to be in tomorrow, the art has to be in on Friday, and the geography the week after. I didn't hear the rest. By the looks of it, she's set for some high marks," replied Tom.

"She's earned it. She works so hard. Is she still going out on Saturday?"

"I think so. Why do women like shopping so much? I always hated it."

"It's fun. And who doesn't want to look good in something new? I always loved getting a new dress. I don't know if I'd like these styles. I'm not sure I have the legs for trousers."

"Or the balance for high heels?"

"I would have liked to have tried, but that will never happen."

"'Twas ever thus." Tom sighed.

"Quite. Anyway, this dress has served me well for years, and corsets are becoming popular again."

There was a knock at the door. All the ghosts froze.

"Come in," said Sarah.

Luke opened the door. Seeing the papers on the floor, he didn't dare venture past the threshold. "I forgot to take the mince out of the freezer. Your brother has suggested we go for an Indian. What do you think?" he asked.

"Sounds good. Give me a few minutes. I'm nearly finished here, then I'll be down," replied Sarah, as she continued to sort papers into piles.

"I thought that was *the* door. I know we're dead, but I nearly had a heart attack," said Tom, wiping his brow. Felicia had picked Mark up when they heard the knock. She now placed him back down on the floor and joined Tom sitting on the end of the bed. "I hope to God if something does happen, it does when we're not here. I don't think we're built for it!"

"No," responded Felicia with a slight laugh. "We're just as likely to run away screaming."

Sarah placed her files into her bag, ready for the next day. She put her shoes on and turned to the dressing table. Without sitting, she leaned in close to check her make-up. Her breath steamed up the mirror in front of her. The two ghosts sitting on the end of the bed noticed nothing out of place, but Sarah did. She breathed out again, harder this time, then pulled away from the mirror. She had seen a single word written on the mirror. *SMUDGE.*

The ghosts watched as she stood for a second looking hard into the mirror at her own reflection. She turned and grabbed her phone off the bed, then left the room without looking back.

"Should be a quiet night tonight," said Tom.

"I think I'll take Mark into the garden for a bit. Will you join us?"

"No, someone should stay. You go, get some fresh air. I'll go later. The sun will be over the house by then and I can sit on the patio. Work on my tan," said Tom, with a sarcastic smile.

Downstairs, Luke stood holding the front door open. "Hurry up! This was your idea."

"I was just finishing a level," replied Oliver, as he raced out of the front room. Felicia and Mark quickly followed before Luke shut the door. He might not have known he was holding it open for them as well, but nevertheless he was. As she passed him Felicia bowed slightly, thanking him for something he had no awareness of. Felicia had been dead for well over a century, but manners still mattered. In the world the dead inhabit, small things always matter, manners being one of them.

In the quiet of the garden Felicia sat on the edge of a step, allowing Mark to wander through the flower beds. She closed her eyes against the sun's rays and breathed in deeply, enjoying the fresh air. It was a cold winter's night for the living, but for the dead it was a glorious summer's day. The air was already warm, but by midnight it would be hot; today would be a scorcher. She slowly stretched out her arms and back. Inside, the door did nothing that could be measured or seen, but it made the dead feel cramped and bound, and the living nervous and unsettled. Its haunting stillness would not last forever; all predators pounce sooner or later. For now, Felicia was out in the fresh air, free from its influence. And she intended to enjoy the peace and solitude, if only for a short time.

Chapter 14

Sarah had a pleasant evening with her brother and father at the Indian restaurant. They had eaten great food, talked about all sorts of things, and laughed a lot. A good tonic for them all. All of Sarah's thoughts on the paranormal had faded into the background. With her mind free of such chains, she felt buoyant and light. When they left the restaurant, she walked tall and proud, as if she were wearing six-inch heels, not trainers.

This sensation lasted until they arrived home. Looking up at her bedroom window, she was brought back down to earth with a bump. Tomorrow lunchtime she would do more research. Her mother had waited long enough. For now, sleep was the priority. All the fun and laughter had been a release, but it had also drained her more than she expected. She hadn't been this happy for some time, but it wasn't enough to stop the rush of important questions from forming in her mind.

She tossed and turned in her sleep. She had had several nights like this since talking to her mother.

Her dreams turned to vivid nightmares. All of them followed the same theme: her mother was in trouble. She was chained, in pain, or being hunted by an unseen force.

The alarm clock went off, waking her violently from a nightmare. Her clothes stuck to her with sweat. Even the sheets were damp with perspiration. She peeled off her clothes in front of the bathroom mirror and threw them straight into the laundry basket. She stopped and looked herself in the eye. She had developed bags under her eyes many months ago, but today they looked more like bin bags. A shower would help wake her up.

Wrapped in a towel, she passed Oliver in the hall – and four ghosts preparing for a shift change. They all looked back at her, at this damp, clearly exhausted young woman. Not saying anything, her gaze fixed on the floor, she went into her room to get dressed.

Uniform on, multiple layers of concealer under her eyes, she was ready to face the day ahead. In her mind she knew what was needed. She put some laundry on, had breakfast, then set out to walk her brother to school. At least she could keep him safe from the bullies on the route to school. Inside school, others would have to take over. Their father knew that Oliver was being bulled, and had talked to the school on several occasions, but this had made things worse for Oliver. Another approach was needed, but Sarah didn't know what to do. This frustrated her.

She was lucky she was at secondary school and had lots of friends around her. They had protected her and given her the support that she needed. From their perspective, all they had done was take her out to get coffee and talked rubbish to her. Their trips to the cinema or the shops had always seemed so normal. That was what she had needed: the normal and the mundane. Giggling about who they fancied or the latest romance between teachers. All of these pointless conversations had helped to keep her grounded through the death of her mother. The trips out and her friends' conversations now helped her grieve. All her friends had seen Amber in her last days, and had attended the funeral. All of them held hands and comforted each other, while wearing a single white rose as instructed. They were good friends. They were all willing to discuss her death, but never lingered on the subject. Everything was kept light and jovial.

Sarah was indeed blessed. Her brother wasn't. His friends didn't really have the ability to help him. They didn't understand how to be around him, so they kept their distance. The death of a parent was something that they refused to accept could happen to them. Therefore, Oliver was odd and out of place, an aberration that was best left alone. The school had done what they could. The teachers were all very supportive, and they had brought in a specialist teaching assistant, one trained in helping a grieving child through the darkness. But there was a limit to what they could achieve. Without friends, he would be forever on the back foot emotionally.

There was hope, however. In a few months he would be joining Sarah at secondary school. The school was already aware of the situation, and was busy planning where best to put him. There were several troubled children who would need support when they started the school. Lumping them together – those who had issues, like Oliver, with those who were in care or who were simply loners – was a simple, but surprisingly effective, solution. Different tutorial groups, but similar classes, was the best way of allowing them to bond with each other naturally, and having contact with others. Luke, Sarah and the staff at both schools had talked about this plan. All had agreed this was a good idea, if Oliver could keep going until it could be put into action.

Having left Oliver at his school gates, Sarah trudged on to hers. Ahead of her she saw the solution. Dan. He was tall and well-muscled for his age, but rugby had scarred his face and hands. He looked like someone who should be avoided at all costs. But his nature was that of a gentle giant. When he had heard of Sarah's loss, he had introduced himself, then given her a bear hug. As well as lifting her off the ground, he had lifted her spirit. He had lost his grandfather, a man he was close to, and he understood all too well what she was going through. He had offered to help in any way he could; all she had to do was to ask.

She sped up to catch up with him, then explained what was happening to Oliver. At once he was on board. He would "have words" with the bullies and "sort them". He might have been gentle to those around him, but he could also impose great fear into those who needed it, a role he took great joy out of. Standing up to bullies was something that he had failed to do until he had grown into himself. Then everyone listened to him!

Morning lessons passed normally. Sarah handed in her coursework to be checked. Then came lunchtime. First Sarah headed to the library; her research was ongoing. She looked up a few things, then bought a couple of bits from a spiritualist site. Then she went to eat and meet Dan.

"Okay, so if I meet you by the small gate, we'll walk back together. Then you can point out the troublemakers," said Dan.

"Yep. Sounds like a plan. Will you talk to them today or leave it for a few?"

"I'll probably leave it until you and Oliver are well out of sight. That way there's no comeback on him."

"Thank you for this. I just can't think of any other way of making them stop."

"Don't worry about it. All I have to do is tell them to stop or else," said Dan. "And don't thank me. I can't think of anything worse than being bullied just because of what happened to your mum. He'll be fine."

Chapter 15

Sarah and Oliver left Dan behind and carried on towards their own house. It wasn't until they got inside that the uncomfortable silence between them had evaporated.

"So, is he your new boyfriend?"

"No. He's just a friend who's also a boy. He's a nice guy, but we aren't right for each other. Do you understand?"

"Nope. But I don't get a lot of things at the moment. Like why are you awake all night?"

"I'm not. I slept right through last night."

"No. Last night you were walking round your room and up and down the stairs at about 3 a.m. I heard you!" said Oliver, not knowing that he had heard the ghosts practising being heard walking up and down.

"Are you sure it wasn't just a dream? I was sound asleep then. It could have been Dad."

"No, I could hear him snoring. It was definitely you. You're not sleepwalking, are you?"

"I suppose I could be. I have been having bad dreams the last few nights," Sarah said. "You used to sleepwalk when you were really little."

"Really? How did it stop?" asked Oliver.

"Mum put a trap down in your doorway. A wet towel. I'll do that tonight, and you tell me if you hear me moving round. Hold on, why are you awake at that time? You promised Dad you wouldn't watch TV too late!" said Sarah.

"I haven't been. I just woke up. You're not the only one having nightmares."

"Do you want to talk about them?"

"No. They'll stop eventually. I just don't want you to fall down the stairs."

"I'll be fine. Right. I'll make the tea, you go start your homework." Sarah switched on the kettle and looked through the cupboards for snacks. Next to the bread bin she spotted a sandwich box. Jackpot! It was half full of chocolate brownies. Just what the doctor ordered.

The two of them sat at the dining table, brownie in one hand, pen in the other, doing homework. The box was quickly emptied and the tea drunk, but at least their homework was also done. Now they could spend the evening doing whatever they wanted.

They both went to their rooms. Oliver put on his games console. He was still struggling with a particular level, while Sarah sat on her bed watching *Mostly Ghostly*. Downstairs, Luke put the supper on and then sat down to watch the first half of the football.

Luke's timing had definitely improved. At the half-time whistle, the food was ready to eat. The three of them sat in front of the TV, waiting for the second half to begin. Sarah wasn't a football fan; the pundit's commentary passed her by with ease. As soon as she had finished eating, she left to start the washing up. Oliver stayed – not because it was his team, but because he was trying to avoid having to dry the dishes.

Upstairs, the two ghosts sat watching the door.

"Right, I've had an idea," said the master.

"What?" asked Felicia.

"We do want to scare her. I know I said before we shouldn't. But the softly-softly method isn't working. And we need that thing gone! And the sooner the better. So, if we scare her a little, she might just start looking at things differently."

"We have all tried to tell her, and so far, nothing. But do we really want to scare the poor girl? And how? I've never been seen or heard. I can, at a push, move something."

"Well, you can do that, but we might have to push things a little further. I think I should show myself.

She doesn't know me, so the thought of a strange man in her room should do it," said the master.

"How come she hasn't heard you? You've been trying. I've watched you," quizzed Felicia.

"I don't know."

"Yes, you do, you know everything. What's going wrong?"

"I've … I've never been heard. There, I said it. Happy now? That's why the family back home named me Bob," said the master, looking at his feet.

"Why didn't you say anything? No one would have minded."

"I was embarrassed. How could I teach others something when I couldn't do it myself?"

"Well, your secret is safe with me. It is very rare for one of us to be heard. We all know that."

"Only because I told you!" said the master.

"How many episodes of *Mostly Ghostly* have we watched? And how often have they had a clear voice that they have heard with their own ears?"

"A few."

"Few and pretty far between! It's a rare gift, and therefore nothing to be ashamed of. But since you obviously don't want me to tell anyone, then I won't. But you do need to stop being so hard on yourself."

"Yes, miss," replied the master, giving a mock salute.

"So, we're going to scare her?" said Felicia in an exasperated manner.

"Yes. I think it will be best if we wait for her to get into bed. Then I'll show myself, then you can push something on the bedside table."

"That sounds alright. We don't have to terrify her, just slightly worry her…"

"Exactly," said the master nervously.

"We'll be fine."

"Of course. We only need to do this once. And it's not like we're the type to get addicted," said the master.

"Exactly. We're good people. We're not that sort. What do we do after?" asked Felicia.

"We watch what she does, and then we take a few shifts off just in case. If she gets too scared, we will need to distance ourselves. And by that, I mean all of us. You, me and everyone back at the mill."

"Right. Are we sure we should do this?" asked Felicia.

"We have to do something. Don't you think?"

"Right, that's the plan. We're in this together," said Felicia, and held out her hand. The master looked Felicia in the eye and shook her hand. They both then returned to sitting in silence, just watching the door. Waiting…

Chapter 16

Having finished cleaning the kitchen by herself, Sarah sat down at the table with a cup of tea. While she drank it, she idly looked through Oliver's workbooks that he had left lying there. As she flipped through the work, she noted the marks. There had been a slight decrease in his work, and then his marks had improved. Looking at the dates, the decrease had been around and after their mother's death. Which was understandable. She placed each book neatly in a pile, then took the rest of her tea upstairs.

At her dressing table she carefully removed her make-up and brushed her hair. She looked at herself. With make-up on, she looked really good. Without it, the stress showed on her face. Her eyes were dark and laden with large bags. She was coming out in spots, which luckily were just small whiteheads. But she had always had perfect skin.

Sarah carefully popped the whiteheads, then set to work with some industrial-strength cleanser. The smell was so strong that she had to take care around her eyes. She had made that mistake once and ended up looking like someone had poked her in both of them.

She rubbed in moisturiser slowly, wondering how Dan had sorted out the bullies. She didn't know him very well at all, but she had confidence that he would. She just didn't know how. Would he threaten them? Would he use physical violence, or just his impressive presence? She had no idea, but hoped that whatever he did it would work. Oliver didn't need to be hassled like this. He had important exams coming up, and he had been through too much already.

Sarah took off her clothes and threw them onto the chair. She got into her snuggly pyjamas and got into bed. She was reading so many textbooks at the moment, she couldn't face the novel she had started, so she turned on her phone.

Sarah was casually flicking though Facebook when her door opened.

"I'm off to bed. I think Dad's going soon," said Oliver.

"Night, night. I hope you get a decent night's sleep."

"Have you put down the trap?" asked Oliver. Sarah had completely forgotten. She had been too preoccupied by other things to worry about the possibility of her sleepwalking.

"Not yet. It's best done just before you go to bed – that way it doesn't dry out. Try and get some sleep. I'll be fine," she said with a smile.

"Good luck, and I'll see you in the morning," he said, closing the door behind him.

Sarah ditched Facebook and played on a couple of apps. An hour passed with surprising ease. Her thoughts focused on finding tricky words or bouncing a ball at the right time. Having used up all of her lives, she turned off her phone and plugged it in to charge. She was just getting out of bed when her phone fell off the bedside table. The thud as it hit the floor made Felicia and the master jump. They were watching the door, not her.

Sarah went to the bathroom and brushed her teeth. In the hallway she passed her father, wished him goodnight and kissed him gently on the cheek. Back in her room she turned off the main light, got into bed and snuggled down to sleep.

She reached out a hand to turn off the bedside lamp, and saw two feet next to the bed. She froze. Slowly, she looked up. Legs, a body in old-fashioned clothes, a man's face. A man she didn't know. She stared at him, and he stared back. She tried to scream, but nothing came out. The man said nothing and did nothing. He just stood there, watching her. Sarah's eyes began to water; she hadn't blinked in a while. Unconsciously she blinked, scared that the man would move during the momentary darkness behind her eyelids. Her eyes opened and he was gone. Was she seeing things? Had she finally gone mad? Who had he been? Sarah was still frozen in the same position. Her breathing was rapid; her heartbeat was through the roof. Was she safe to turn the light off? Was she safe to move? Should she get help or hide under the covers? All these thoughts whizzed through her head at a million miles an hour. She pulled her hand back under the covers and drew them up so only her eyes were visible. It's fair to say she was terrified.

She realised how fast her breathing was, and tried to calm herself down with a few deep breaths. The hot air ricocheted off the covers and back onto her face. Her breathing started to slow. Sarah peeked out from underneath the covers and looked round the empty room. As she let out a huge sigh, the bedside light turned off. Sarah's head whipped around. In the darkness, there was nothing visible. Tentatively she reached out once more and turned on the lamp. Still nothing. But the light was a sudden and welcome friend. She left it on, and then took one more look around the room. Reluctantly she turned over in bed and closed her eyes.

"Well, I didn't hear you. I guess the trap worked then," said Oliver.

Sarah hadn't noticed him come into the kitchen, so jumped when he started talking.

"No. I didn't wake up on the towel, so I guess I didn't sleepwalk last night," replied Sarah. She was still shaky. She had spent hours frozen in one position, too afraid to move or even open her eyes. She lay there just listening to the sounds of the house as it settled. Sarah couldn't say how long she had slept, or even if she had slept at all. She felt like she had been awake all night.

"You alright? You seem a bit jumpy," said her dad. He had clearly spotted her reaction. "What's this about sleepwalking?"

"It's nothing. Oliver thinks he heard me moving around during the night a few times. I don't remember anything. I think it's just his imagination. I doubt I'm sleepwalking," replied Sarah.

"I take it the trap was a wet towel by the door?"

"Yep. But I slept through." As Sarah said this, she suddenly thought about that man. Could Oliver have heard him moving around? He had looked huge as he stared down at her. Who was he? Was he what had scared her mum? Sarah badly wanted to tell her dad about what the man, but she was scared that he would think she had gone mad or was hallucinating. So she kept quiet and put on a fake smile to reassure him.

"You two had better go or you'll be late. Are you alright to do that pasta bake tonight?"

"Yes. Bye Dad." Sarah raced out of the house, ahead of Oliver. She wasn't running to get to school as much as she was running from the thought of that man. Was he watching her all the time? She had got dressed quickly for fear of being watched by some perverted ghost. She would have to get rid of him; he clearly wasn't nice. He had to be the danger her mother had written about on the Ouija board.

She knew what she had to do.

Chapter 17

The sun had set on the mill and the handful of ghosts assembled there. William, Nat and Claire remained unconscious and draped in the water of the stream. All of them had seemed to have built up a tolerance to the energy of this healing water. During the first few days, they had to be turned at least twice an hour. Now, several weeks later, it was only once or twice all night.

Mark raced as fast as he could, crawling on his hands and knees, to greet Felicia. The two of them looked exhausted from the day's adventure.

"What's happened?"

"Why are you all back?

"Who's watching the door?" asked Tom and Ethan in quick succession.

"We decided that we have to change tack. Sarah wasn't going to hear any of us. So, we scared her a little bit," said the master.

"How much is a little bit?" asked Ethan.

"Hopefully enough to get her to smudge the house. She's seen them doing it on that *Mostly Ghostly* programme. She's bright, so she'll know what to do. But…" The master looked at Felicia in the fading light.

"But if she is really scared, we can't risk anyone becoming addicted. Or being banished from the house. So we—" said Felicia.

The master interrupted. "So we think it best if we leave the house alone for a few days, just in case. The door hasn't done anything while we've been watching it."

"And how are you both feeling after scaring Sarah?" asked Ethan.

The master and Felicia looked at each other and said at the same time, "Guilty." With that simple word, they knew that there wasn't a risk of them getting addicted to the negative feelings they had caused in Sarah.

"But what if she doesn't smudge? She could open the door without realising it," Tom said.

"That's true, but she has a good idea of what to do – or she should have. And look what happened last time that door opened," said the master, looking at the three comatose ghosts. "We can't risk anyone else being hurt by that thing."

"What do we do now? Just wait here and hope she doesn't release a demon?" asked Tom.

"No. We watch the house from the top of the road. Meanwhile, I will go to the city and see if some of my old friends are able to help. If nothing else, we need more hands on deck," replied the master

"How long has it been since you went to the city?" asked Felicia.

"I admit it's been a while, but they're good people. And I know where they have their meetings," said the master with a wry smile. "It'll be fine, dear, trust me."

As soon as the sun began to creep above the horizon of the dead night, three ghosts left the mill. Ethan and Stan went to stand guard at the end of William's road, while the master walked through the small town and out the other side towards the city.

"Is this close enough?" asked Ethan.

"I think we can sit on that wall without being too close," replied Stan, pointing to an obliging wall.

"I know we are some distance away, but I can still feel it. Can you?"

"Yep. That thing's potent in all the wrong ways," said Stan.

Over the next few days the guard continued, both at the mill and on William's street. The daily comings and goings of its residents were monitored, but the focus was always on William's house. Who had been there, when they had left, had any post been delivered?

"Morning. How are you both doing?" asked Tom.

"All quiet on the Western Front. Since they got home, nothing's happened," Felicia replied.

"They got a parcel earlier. Sarah signed for it, so it's probably hers," said Ethan.

"Any idea what was in it?" Stan asked.

"Nope, but it didn't look like DVDs or books. It looked light but was quite big," replied Ethan, holding out his hands to indicate the size of the parcel. "About A4, I'd say, but full."

"I wonder what was in it. Could it have been a smudging stick?" asked Tom.

"It's possible. But we didn't want to get a closer look, just in case," answered Felicia. "What's the news from the mill?"

"Nothing yet. The three are still out of it, and there's still no sign of the master," said Stan.

"The cat still hanging around?" Tom had quite a soft spot for the cat. And going by his behaviour, the feeling was mutual.

With no warning, a wave of energy blew past the ghosts, knocking them off their feet. With no clue what had happened, they slowly picked themselves up off the ground. Shock was clearly visible on their faces.

"What the hell was that? asked Ethan.

"No clue," said Stan as he helped Felicia up.

"What do we do?" asked Tom.

Felicia looked around. Nothing visible had changed, so she knew it had to be something inside the house. "Stan, you and Ethan go back to the mill, make sure everyone is okay. Tom and I will go inside to find out if the door is active or not."

No one argued, but acted on her instructions immediately. Tom took Felicia's hand, while they both looked directly at the house. Knowing something inside had changed made it feel more imposing than before. It was such a strange feeling. That house had always felt so warm and welcoming, despite the family's woes. Felicia's fear was that the new door that had formed would stay forever, or would get worse. It could open.

The two ghosts let go of each other's hands as they began to walk towards the house. They passed through the front door. Cautiously, they looked around. Nothing seemed out of place. Without checking all of the downstairs, they headed up to Sarah's room. As they stepped onto the landing, they were hit by the strong smell of burning herbs. The smell got stronger with each step they took across the landing and down the hall.

Inside her room, Sarah was opening the window to let out the smoke that filled the air. On the dressing table, a stick of sage was in a glass of water. Charred pieces of sage floated on the surface of the water, while heavier pieces slowly drifted down to the bottom. After seeing the warning on the mirror, Sarah had found a smudging stick online and read a detailed guide to performing this ritual. The fear that drove her was the image of the man standing over her bed.

"She's done it – she's smudged!" said Tom.

"But it hasn't worked; the door is still here."

"Maybe it's sealed and it won't open now?"

"We can but hope," replied Felicia.

BANG, BANG, BANG. Both ghosts jumped out of their skin. The bangs had come from the door.

"It's not done that before!" said Tom nervously as he backed away.

"That is not a good sign."

Chapter 18

Eyes wide open, William couldn't make out anything past the dazzling sunshine. Slowly he sat up. Looking down at himself; he realised that one of his feet was wet from the stream. All around him were the others, all trying to get up from the damp grass.

"Oh my God! You're awake. Are you okay?" asked the old woman.

"I think so. What happened?" replied William.

"No idea, dear. But you've all been out for nearly a month!"

"A month? That's not possible."

"Afraid so. Just take things slowly," said the old woman, turning her attention to the others.

William slowly began to focus on his surroundings. He knew where they were, but he had no idea how they had got there. Claire and Nat were both apparently in a similar condition to himself.

"Are you alright?" William asked.

"I think so," replied Claire, who was closest to William.

"Looks like someone has missed me!" said Nat. Mark was bouncing on him with a huge grin on his face. Having given Nat several hugs and kisses, he crawled off in the direction of Claire and William, then greeted them both in the same way. A broad smile, hugs and kisses for them both. None of them had any idea what had happened since they left the house. Regardless, it still felt good to be dead!

Nat had slowly followed Mark to the others. When he reached them, he kissed Claire, then hugged her deeply, despite the bouncing child on her lap. With only a vague notion that time had passed, it felt like an age since he last held his lover. This was the best medicine, and just what he needed. William joined in the group hug, kissing Mark then Nat on the forehead. He and Claire kissed each other on the cheek, then hugged as only long-lost family can. All the others could do was to watch as the four ghosts embraced.

"Is that who I think it is?" asked Claire. She could see several figures coming towards them. One was in a Santa suit...

"What happened? My goodness, you're awake. How do you feel?" questioned the master.

"Sarah used a Ouija board. Something tried to come through, but me and Nat held the door closed. Claire got her to stop," replied William.

"Hidden talents, this one!" Nat smiled as he kissed Claire once more.

"Then we just woke up here. How long have we been out?" asked William.

"Too long, if you ask me. Does everything work?" asked the master, as he helped William to stand.

"I'm a bit stiff, but I think so. What have we missed?"

"Loads," replied the old woman.

The three victims were made to sit back down while the master told them what had been happening. He was just introducing the two ghosts who had joined him, when Ethan and Stan arrived, out of breath and panting, their faces shocked.

"You're awake? Something's happened at the house. We think Sarah has tried smudging! It blew us off our feet!" said Ethan.

"Us too."

"That must have got rid of that bloody door," said the master. "But we had better wait and find out."

"These things can backfire," said Pa.

*

He was right. The door hadn't opened again, but the sound of knocking from the other side was bad enough. Felicia and Tom were both glued to the spot, both too afraid to move. *BANG BANG BANG.*

"Can we risk leaving it to get help?" asked Tom.

"Don't you mean, can we risk staying?" responded Felicia. Their eyes were fixed on the door.

"I think we had better leave well alone. I don't want to find out what's behind there, and I wouldn't know what to do if I did."

Felicia looked at Tom. He took her hand once more, then they ran for it – down the stairs and out of the front door, up the road and around the corner. Felicia had gathered her long skirts in one hand, revealing her bloomers, something she was always careful to conceal. In this instance, modesty was the last thing on her mind. They ran as fast as they could along the main road, not bothering to avoid the traffic or the living walking along the pavement. Neither of them stopped or even slowed until they had reached the mill.

"Ah, here is Mr Thomas and our dearest Felicia. May I introduce Pa and Simon" said the master calmly.

Felicia dropped her skirts to shake their hands. Tom was preoccupied with more important matters to worry about social niceties.

"She did smudge, but it's woken up the door – or, rather, what's behind it!" he tried to say, despite his breathlessness.

"What! Do you mean it's woken it up?" asked Simon.

"It banged loudly three times, twice. Something is behind it and it wants out!" replied Felicia. "Good grief, you're awake!" she added, as she spotted the three victims standing behind the newcomers.

"That's not good," said Ethan.

"No. We had better go and see what's going on. Who's coming?" asked the master.

"I will," said Nat.

"It's my house, so count me in," said William.

"I'd rather not," said Felicia as she continued to straighten her skirts.

"Count me out, that thing's unpleasant," said Tom.

"Okay, we'll go and work out what to do next," said the master.

They nodded in agreement. The group who were brave enough or stupid enough to go then left to examine the scene. The others sat down with heavy sighs. A lot had happened in a very short space of time. Even though they had no need to breathe regularly, they all felt the need to catch their breath. The two things are very different, and not something that you really notice when you are alive.

But when you are dead, you can go hours without taking a breath. The dead only really need to breathe when they are straining physically or when talking. So to feel the need to breathe deeply and repeatedly was something that couldn't and shouldn't be ignored.

The remaining group of ghosts sat in silence, soaking up the sun's rays while trying to comprehend recent events. But Tom was so shaken by the banging on the door that he paced nervously up and down, rubbing his head and interlocking his fingers. To a behaviourist, this need to touch yourself is a sure sign that a person is feeling very anxious and needs reassurance. Given what they had heard, and the nightmare scenarios going through his head, it was obvious that he needed reassurance. However, without an expert's assessment of the situation, all they could do was sit and worry. Imagining what lurked behind that door filled them all with absolute dread.

The only person who seemed to be at ease with the situation was Mark. He had spent the last few weeks quietly moving from victim to victim, sitting still and pensive for hours, just watching them sleep. He had never reached the talking stage, so it was difficult to tell what went through his tiny head. But to the keen observer, it was obvious that he had deep thoughts. The silent babe was now quite lively, as he moved from lap to lap.

He was all smiles and hugs for Felicia and Claire. She was the only victim who had opted to stay. He brimmed with love for the two women in their moment of fear and crisis. The warm hugs he gave helped to slow the thoughts that were speeding through their heads. None of these thoughts were good; they were all worst-case scenarios connected with that door.

Chapter 19

The master, Simon, Pa, Ethan, William and Nat walked at a steady pace towards the house. Panic would have made them stop; fear would have made them turn around and leave. They all felt the presence of the house long before it came into view. To the living, it merely felt slightly uneasy. To the dead, a low hum emanated from its very foundations. There was a real power to it, and it was far from good. Evil, pure evil, was everywhere.

As they rounded the corner, each ghost got the same feeling: the feeling of being totally unwelcome. But that wasn't something that could be ignored or shrugged off. This was stronger, and not just tangible, but here, there, everywhere you looked. There was no running from it. Either you faced it head on, or you ran and hid.

All the ghosts were strong in themselves; very little could scare any of them. Yet as they got to the front gate, they all stopped. None of them wanted to be the first in. William brought up the rear. This was his house; it had been his home. Even with another family living there, it still felt like home. Now it felt like a stranger's house. A stranger who would kill you as soon as look at you.

William pulled himself up to his full height, then calmly walked through the ghosts as they stood looking at the building. He might have seemed calm, even brave. But deep down he was terrified of what was in there.

He had died a long time ago. Hundreds of years ago, in fact. But right here and now, all he had seen and experienced faded to nothing. He had never had to deal with something like this before. He had heard rumours, even brushed past these events, but he had never faced them. Until now he had always run, leaving the horrors and fears behind him as he moved on.

The guilt of his cowardice engulfed him. For whatever reason, be it his love of his home or his love for his new family, he found the strength to face this. Without stopping, he crossed the threshold and marched up the stairs towards the bedroom. The others followed, quietly and cautiously.

The living were all safely tucked up in bed, warm and snug against the cold night air. The dead were blessed with a hot sunny day. Entering the room, the light streamed through the closed curtains, illuminating everything, including the door.

William's heart sank as he saw that the door remained. But without slowing, he moved towards the bed. Sarah was fast asleep. Only her head poked out from under the covers. She was peaceful and at ease. Yet the ultimate predator sat just a few feet away from her, just behind the door she had summoned. William learned over and kissed her on the forehead. She didn't move. This gentle expression of love and care went unnoticed.

"Is she okay?" asked the master.

"Seems to be," replied William. "So what do you think about that thing?" he asked Simon, who was the expert on such matters. Or at least, he had the most experience of them. Simon stood in front of the door, pondering it.

"It's a door to hell alright." He stepped closer and ran a finger along the frame. "And it's active – look, it's started dripping. You were right to guard it. Did any of you touch this thing?"

"Me and William did when it first opened," replied Nat.

"I told everyone to watch it, but not to touch it, just in case," said the master.

"Good. You two are lucky to be dead. A door like this could easily have killed you. That's why you all passed out – it was the power of this that did that." He paused and backed away from the door.

"What happens now?" asked William.

"Is she the one that summoned it? She has tried smudging, you say?" asked Simon.

"Yes, but apparently that didn't work," replied the master.

"Well, the good news is that the door is sealed, but what's behind it is clearly awake and wants out. If she's dumb enough to try a Ouija board again, that thing will get out. We can't open it, but the power coming off it will mess with your head, if you let it." He turned and faced the door once more. "Two-man shifts – one shift on, two off. If we are lucky, only we will know that thing is here. No one touches it. And we will have to try and get her to do the smudging again. Only she can get rid of it properly."

The group nodded in agreement. This was still dangerous. Before, the door had felt like a predator ready to pounce, but even predators can be deterred. The door was now a bomb, ready to go off at a moment's notice.

Silence filled the bedroom. Had Sarah been awake, even she would have felt the stillness that encapsulated the room. The sort of stillness you get just before an earthquake, powerful and fleeting. There one second and gone the next. But the sort of second that seems to last for minutes, if not hours.

The door remained, looking even more imposing than ever.

The group split. Simon and Ethan stayed to stand guard, while the others made their way back to the mill, to tell the rest what had to be done.

The next few days passed quickly. With all the ghosts working shifts, they had very little time for fun. No more trips to the cinema or nightclub. All any of them had the energy to do was hang around the mill when they weren't guarding the door.

Spending any time with the door made them feel ill. The ghosts would leave after a shift feeling exhausted. They would spend their shift standing guard, watching, waiting. By the end of a shift, their nerves were shot. The gnawing pit in their stomach would begin to physically hurt after a few hours in the presence of the door. The physical strain was nothing to the physiological. Hours spent in relative silence didn't help. Some of the dead talk rapidly when they are nervous. But the fear that this door emanated stopped that. The door and what lay behind it seemed to seep into their very souls. Every waking thought was about it. Idle thoughts about the sunny day outside vanished before the thoughts of a demon.

Only Simon and Pa had ever seen a demon. Both of them were happy to talk to the others, but when they were asked about their past experiences, they clammed up. Pa admitted that the demon he had run into was a different one to the one Simon had dealt with. But he was vague on any other details.

This lack of knowledge didn't help. Unconsciously they all imagined the beast. William couldn't decide if it had a tail, or horns, or gnashing teeth. The image didn't matter; what mattered was that this was real and here. And there was no running this time. If he did, he would never be able to return home. He would never be able to look himself in the eye if he left his family with this.

William's dead family were amazing, and he loved them with all his heart. As he sat on the bed, he resigned himself to his fate. If he had to give his life to save them, he would. He knew that they were more than prepared to do the same for him. As for his living family, they remained unaware of him, but that was okay. Watching them struggle, then begin to recover, he had grown attached to them all. He had grown to like other families over the years, but not like this. This was different. He loved them like they were family. Those feelings grew with each day he spent with them.

Yet again all the ghosts tried to communicate with Sarah. Sadly, as before, their messages fell on deaf ears. All their attention was firmly fixed on this broken family. But seeing how they were starting to heal themselves gave the ghosts hope that anything could be achieved. They all had their favourites, it's true. But they all cared deeply for this family. The master had a soft spot for Oliver, but greatly admired Luke. Both had their good and bad points, but that didn't matter. The family were good people who had been dealt a bad hand. They faced everything with a smile and a deep determination to overcome.

Simon and Pa were new to this messed-up family, yet even they were rapidly falling for them. If the living had any idea how much the dead cared for them, they might see the world differently. Sadly, only a few individuals are blessed with this knowledge.

Of course, there are exceptions to this. Being looked after by friendly spirits is a good thing, but if a spirit that isn't friendly comes into your life – well, that's another matter entirely…

One morning William and Claire were walking towards the house when they thought they saw a hellion. Every hellion William had seen had looked the same. As their addiction to negative feelings grew, their appearance became rougher. They all had messy hair, torn clothes and a wildness in their eyes that made his stomach turn.

The dead don't tend to refer to themselves as ghosts, just people. Which, after all, is what they are. The only real difference between the living and the dead is their impact on the world around them. The living have the biggest impact, that's obvious. Even those shut inside due to illness leave their mark. Maybe not as large, but it's still there for all to see. The dead, however, rarely make an impression. Individuals like Pa are an exception, and are praised and envied for their deeds.

"Are you okay?" asked Pa.

"We think we saw a hellion on our way here…" replied William as he continued to watch out of the front window, hardly aware of Pa and Ethan.

Pa and Ethan looked at each other in shock. This was not what they wanted to hear.

Chapter 20

"Hellion Noun. N. Amer. *colloq*. A mischievous or troublesome person, especially a child. Perhaps from dialect *hallion* 'a worthless fellow', changed by association with hell." Oxford English Dictionary.

William and Felicia had been walking towards the house when they saw someone looking at it. He was standing in the garden of a neighbouring house, his back to them.

"Who's that? I don't recognise them," said William.

"No idea. Hello! You there, can you hear me?" called Felicia. With that, the man bolted up the path and round the side of the house. William was hot on his heels, but couldn't keep up. William burst into the back garden. One of the children who lived there was having a birthday party. Between the balloons, screaming children and various parents, William was unable to see where the strange person had gone.

With care, and as much speed as possible, he hunted his quarry through the excited crowd. But to no avail. It was a bright spring day for the living, but for the dead it was a damp autumn night. With little moonlight to aid him, it was an impossible task.

"Did you catch him?" asked Felicia.

"No, I lost him. You don't think that was a hellion, do you?"

"I hope not. We've got enough problems without one of them."

"We had better get to our shift," said William.

In the house, Pa and Ethan were watching the door. William didn't even go into the bedroom. Instead he took up his post on the landing. From this window, he could see the whole street. Hoping he would see the intruder, he decided to sit and watch for the whole shift.

A hellion is not a pleasant prospect. Having one in your house is even less so. In the TV show *Mostly Ghostly*, they call these spirits demons or poltergeists. Hellion is a term the spirit world uses. Put simply, they used to be your normal, average ghosts. In life, they were just as normal. But then they go bad. Invariably, they get a taste for causing the living harm in some way. The negative emotions they give off are highly addictive, and often fatal to the ghost.

In the normal course of events, the dead's clothes don't change, or even wear out. But when an individual becomes addicted to causing the living harm, and becomes a hellion, their clothes start to disintegrate. The hellion begins to look as unkempt on the outside as they are on the inside. It's normally a never-ending spiral downwards. Deeper and deeper into the addiction, until the end, when they burn up.

It's not just the high that they get that makes these emotions so addictive. The ghost causing the harm tends to learn how to do things quicker than most spirits. The master, even after being dead for centuries, hasn't yet learned how to be heard. Yet a ghost of only a few months that has become a hellion could have perfected this, and many more skills, making a potent and very dangerous combination.

William was a definite film fan. Even though he had learned to read, films were always better in his mind. He had known about hellions for some time when he first saw the *Star Wars* films. He was surprised to hear Yoda telling Luke that the dark side was quicker and easier than the good. He knew the writers had no knowledge of hellions, yet here on the big screen this concept was being portrayed as fiction. Make-believe for the living, maybe, but a stark reality for the dead.

"If you two are alright here, we'll head off to the mill. Simon and the master will know what to do with one of those guys," said Pa.

Nothing fazed this man. Even with the prospect of a vicious addict in the vicinity, he still smiled. To him there was always hope, regardless of the situation and those involved.

It was an odd pair that walked away from the house that day. A cheerful man in a Santa suit and a pessimist dressed in a traditional butcher's outfit. William watched as they walked up the hill away from him. They looked so bizarre that even William, who had in his time seen some very strange things, laughed at the thought of this odd couple.

Pa and Ethan got on, and as they left the influence of the door behind them were able to start laughing, helped by Pa's unyielding sense of humour. As they crossed the threshold out of the house, it came back to life.

"Cheer up, lad. What goes from green to red at the flick of a switch?"

"No idea," said Ethan.

"A frog in a blender," replied Pa. "What do you call an MP on the moon?"

"Pass."

"Lost! What do you call a dozen MPs on the moon?"

"Lost?" replied Ethan.

"A problem." Pa chuckled. "What do you call all the MPs in the world on the moon?"

"I don't know!" Ethan giggled.

"Problem solved!" replied Pa, bursting into laughter. His jokes were bad, but they were a good sort of bad. And they always did what they were intended to do: make people laugh or at least smile, if only at how cheesy they were. Many of his favourites must have come out of Christmas crackers. But in fairness, he was the embodiment of all things Christmas.

Most people would have taken Pa as they saw him – as an old man who looked and acted like a typical Father Christmas – but they would have been wrong. Behind the jolly facade he was a very clever man. Telling jokes was just his way of getting people to relax. Once that happened, they normally began to open up about themselves.

Pa might not have all the answers, but he knew people. It's not who you know, it's how you know them. After they had opened up to him, Pa saw them as family. And when he was faced with a problem, if he couldn't solve it himself, he would know someone who could. He was never afraid to ask for help; at an early age he had realised how people were pleased to be asked if they could do something. Let's face it, everyone likes to show off sometimes. Even if it is a relatively simple task. This was his hidden talent, and he used it to his advantage.

Chapter 21

Simon, in life, had lived and worked on his family's pig farm on the other side of town. Oddly enough, it wasn't the pigs that had killed him, but the war – well, that's what he claimed. During the early days of the Great War, he and his father had been left to manage a large farm without any help. The young men the farm employed had all eagerly signed up to serve.

A few weeks before the women from the newly formed Women's Land Army arrived, Simon had been handling their large cob. Normally a gentle giant, the horse worked as hard as everyone else. But, unlike the farmers, he was well cared for. The best hay and food were set aside for him. At the end of the day he was brushed down and given a rug to keep him warm in his stable. But that day, everyone's tempers were frayed. Overworked and tired, something had to give. Normally this horse was steady and solid; he stood proud and tall while his harness was put on. But that day he was different, as they all were. Simon was putting on his tack when a strap slipped off and landed on the floor. There was nothing unusual about that, so Simon bent down to pick it up and reattach it. But as he bent down, the horse was spooked by something, and kicked out. He caught Simon square in the chest.

The blow from this big horse was catastrophic. Simon was dead before he hit the ground. It was several minutes before someone found his lifeless body. The horse knew instantly that something was wrong and had begun gently nudging his loving owner, but it was too late.

Before Simon died, he hadn't believed in ghosts. After all, their house was old, but he had never experienced any ghostly activity. Ghosts were just in stories. Given the stunning revelation that they were real, and he was now one of them, he had gone out into the world to find out all he could. He had faced – and dealt with – hellions, demons and everything in between. But he still hadn't cracked the ultimate mystery: why some people linger and others move on. The consensus was that it depended on the individual and how they had died. But most ghosts believed that they had some sort of unfinished business. Some, like William, who had been raised in a religious family, believed that this was purgatory.

With the new-found knowledge, Simon had returned home. Living there was his nephew's family. On the surface it seemed that very little had changed, except the horse. Years had passed; the Great War and the Second World War were over. The farm had survived through innovation.

Machines had taken over from the horse. The pigs were still well looked after, but they were more intensively farmed.

His brother Luke had been a boy when Simon had died, Simon being older by a good ten years. The boy had grown into a man, but had retained his love of the new. As a child, Luke had always been fascinated by adverts for the latest tractor, or the newest invention. Their father, on the other hand, hated all things new. The old ways were best, because they had served him and countless generations before him. But the dawning of a new era in farming had come just when Luke had taken over. He had breathed new life into the old farm and made it very successful.

When Simon had died, had been young and full of life. When Simon returned, however, he saw the ravages of time written all over his brother. He was old, crippled and bowed, unable to walk without a stick, yet still involved in the running of the business. Simon had wanted so badly to tell him how proud he was of all that he had achieved. But there was a problem. He tried for all he was worth to communicate, but the only people who noticed his presence were his nephew's wife and children.

The children weren't scared, but their mother was. Not for herself, but for her children. In a moment of desperation, she had spoken to the local vicar. He was an old-school priest, self-taught in the art of exorcisms, and keen to practise this ancient Christian rite.

He had little experience, but he certainly had the knack. He had come to the house with holy water and crucifixes. Walking around the house and then the farm, he had blessed every possible corner. With every flick of his wrist, he sprinkled holy water, pushing Simon out of his own home. Unable ever to return, he had left with a heavy heart and a beaten soul. He had heard of his brother's passing from another ghost who was passing through. The fact that he hadn't lingered was a blessing, but not being able to say goodbye nearly broke Simon, this once proud man.

So he spent his days in the city, away from his memories of his former home. He had begun to heal. And rather than simply knowing people, he found he had family around him, and his true calling: helping the living deal with the nasty elements of the spirit world.

"Are they sure it was a hellion?" Simon asked Pa.

"I don't know. They didn't get a clear look at him," Pa replied.

"William's put himself on the landing so he can try and spot him again. If it is a hellion, than they're bound to show up again," said Ethan.

"What do we do if it is a hellion? How can we stop one of them?" asked Stan.

"*Should* we stop them, would be a better question," replied Simon. "They said his clothes looked tattered. Only hellions look like that. We need to get Sarah to smudge again, and to do it properly. A hellion is a nasty prospect, but you said Sarah tried to smudge after you and Felicia scared her. Maybe it's just what we need?"

"We can't just throw a hellion at them and hope they're okay! What are you thinking, man? That would be cruel," objected the master.

"Cruel, yes, but effective. We can't get through to her, so we have to think outside the box. She watches that TV show, and in my experience, people don't put up with hellions for too long. Not in this day and age," said Simon. "Once she smudges, she will rid the house of the hellion – and the door."

"Well, you're the expert. If you think we should do nothing, then I have to agree with you," said the master. "Do we all agree?"

Most of the ghosts present nodded in agreement; except Tom.

"I think this could do more harm than good," said Tom.

"Give it a few days. We still don't know for certain if it was a hellion the others saw," Simon replied. "And if it is, and Sarah smudged the first time after she was scared, then she should smudge again, and Sarah will be able to get rid of them both."

Reluctantly Tom agreed. The logic was sound, but the thought of letting a hellion near this family weighed on his conscience. Simon realised the person with the biggest problem wasn't even here.

William loved this family, and he would do anything he could to protect them, especially the children. But if he was prepared to do whatever was needed, then he could be talked into following this plan of action. And he was.

Simon and William spoke at length about the merits of this plan and the possible repercussions. Simon reassured him that there was a back-up plan if all else failed, but he wouldn't say exactly what that involved. They both realised that, should the hellion start on the family, it wouldn't take Sarah long to realise that something had gone wrong, and that the smudging would have to be redone. Therefore, there was minimal risk to them, and hopefully they would soon be rid of that door.

Banishing the door had to be their prime concern, as it posed the greatest risk. A hellion could make the family's life hell, that was true, but a demon would kill them. The door was sealed but it could, by dint of a mistake, be unlocked. The chance of a demon wandering their peaceful town was a risk none of them wanted to take. Too many lives would be at risk: both the living and the dead would be vulnerable. The difference between a hellion and a demon was vast. The hellion could, at worst, be described as an angry drunk. Its potential for violence was evident, but it was more of a nuisance than a definite threat, only really capable of scaring the living. By contrast, the demon was a fully fledged psychopath, schooled in the art of killing and with the overwhelming need to do so. This was the real threat they faced.

Demons don't die by normal means; destroying one is almost impossible. On the other hand, a hellion has a limited lifespan. Time would catch up with it sooner rather than later. If the demon was in any way powerful or experienced, it could spend years in the town. It could kill off their family of ghosts one by one, leaving the living with no one to protect them.

On the TV show *Mostly Ghostly* they had tried to investigate one such entity. They discovered that the thing that stalked the family was death incarnate. Various members of the family had died from seemingly normal afflictions. But they had passed in quick succession. The finger of blame pointed firmly at a demon.

A simple hellion would have scared them, and they would have been excited by the evidence obtained. Sadly, that wasn't the case. The demon attacked without hesitation, leaving two members of the crew with deep cuts and a third with a burn like a brand. The thought of a full night's investigation was abandoned; the risk to the crew was too great. The show ended with them recommending a full exorcism of the house.

Sarah had watched this episode several times. The silent ghosts who watched with her were forced to view what could potentially happen to them all. Sarah and the ghosts all recognised this potential threat; it chilled them to the core.

But there is a big difference between watching these attacks on TV and experiencing them in real life. Sarah had been scared by the man standing over her bed, but since she had smudged she hadn't felt any odd presences. She was a little jumpy, but things felt calmer. Even Oliver was doing better without his bullies, and that was all that mattered right now.

Chapter 22

Sarah was busily writing up a piece of coursework on the Great War. Not the most cheerful subject matter, but her paper was focusing on the Christmas Day truce. She was trying, and failing, to get a photo of the actual football to fit among the testimonies and her own analysis. But the photo continued to put itself where it wanted to be, and not where she wanted it to be.

"He's still outside. That damn hellion should have made a move by now," Simon said as he entered the room.

"He'll come in when he's ready. When he does, will we have to keep guard all the time or should we just leave him to it?" asked Felicia.

"I think we leave him to it, and just watch from outside. Being banished isn't a comfortable experience. When she does it, whoever is in the house will be banned for the rest of their death, so we need to make sure William isn't here. I wouldn't want him to go through what I did," replied Simon.

"Do you miss them that badly?" asked Felicia.

"Yes. I just want to see the house again. I don't know my nephew's family – I haven't watched them grow up or spent much time with them. But I'd like to see my house again," Simon said solemnly.

"Maybe when we're done with this debacle, one of us could go there for you, tell you what things look like? It would give you an idea of how they are doing."

"Could do… This thing still makes my stomach churn," he said, looking at the door.

"I think it will until it's gone. Did you hear? Pa heard Sarah say the wall looked damp. I wonder what that means."

"It means the demon behind it is gearing up, ready to come through. The living normally notice weird patches of mould – she's very observant. Most don't notice the damp first."

"And yet she's unaware of us being here, or that there's a bloody door to hell here. What do you think of the coursework?" asked Felicia.

"Not bad. But I only heard about the truce; I wasn't there, and never met anyone that was. But it is well thought out, and I like the way she's mixed in bits of her psychology work. That definitely helps. She should get top marks."

"And if she doesn't, are you going to haunt the offending teacher?" joked Felicia.

"No, but I will be inwardly very disappointed in them. I find it endlessly reassuring that we hate being here with that thing, yet Mark doesn't seem in the least bit affected."

"He just loves being here. He is very fond of this place. He is quieter, but he still wants to come here." The two ghosts sat and watched as Mark continued to investigate the broken mirror. Sarah had found a replacement mirror for the frame. Ethan and Thomas had spent a pleasant shift watching Sarah carefully take out the broken pieces of glass that remained in the frame. Then with even more care she tacked in the new glass. They agreed that she had the skills to perform such a delicate task.

"It looks antique, that," said Simon.

"I think so. The house where I worked had one very similar, but it was bought brand-new then."

"So that would make it – what? One hundred and fifty years old?"

"Around that."

"What year is it?"

"It's 2019 now, so yes, around that, give or take a few years," replied Felicia.

An almost comfortable silence fell between them. Just Sarah's gentle tapping on the computer and the low music coming from her phone could be heard. The rest of the house was empty and still. Luke and Oliver were out doing some shopping, so that Sarah had some peace and solitude to finish her coursework. Despite the presence of three others in the room, she felt alone. At one with her thoughts, she was able to type quickly; she had spent a lot of time thinking about what to write and how best to do it. Now in the peace of her room she could let it out.

After around half an hour, Sarah stopped typing. She changed her position on the bed. Stretching out her legs, she began to reread and check her work. Unknowingly, she was flanked by Felicia and Simon, both of them eager to read what she had written.

When William learned to read, he, like many others, struggled. Not with the lessons, but with the darkness. He had spent many months in a junior school leaning over pupils learning how to sound out his words, craning to see the pages in the dim moonlight that came in through an obliging window. One girl in particular was positioned perfectly, her chair and table being closest to the window and the light. However, it soon became apparent that she could tell that someone was looking over her shoulder. After a few minutes she would start to cover her book with her body.

William nevertheless learned to read and was soon reading books that the older children were reading, and so he didn't have to follow this child any more. For the vast majority of older ghosts, this was how they had learned to read. With little or no education in life, they had to learn after they had died.

Having checked over her work and corrected the odd spelling mistake, Sarah put the laptop down and left the room. She returned a few minutes later with a cup of tea and a couple of biscuits from the barrel. She added a few more corrections, then closed down the program and began to watch a *Mostly Ghostly* episode. Still flanked by Felicia and Simon, the titles rolled.

"Come on, Mark, you'll like this." Felicia beckoned to Mark. He quickly crawled across the floor to join them. Normally he would have sat with Felicia, but he was clearly becoming fond of Simon, so he joined him instead. Simon sat on the floor, while Mark stood on his lap. With all of them able to see clearly, calmness filled the room.

BANG BANG BANG

"Oh, do shut up, we're trying to listen. I can't wait for that thing to go!" replied Felicia. Despite her objections, the calmness was gone. The three ghosts unconsciously shifted in their seats, alert and ready for action, yet trying to remain relaxed. It seemed to be an impossible task.

After some time, movements downstairs indicated the arrival of Luke and Oliver. Sarah paused the episode and left to speak to them.

"How did you get on?" Sarah asked her father.

"Okay. But no one had the biscuit things you asked for. I did find this." Luke pulled out a folded piece of paper from his back pocket and gave to Sarah. "I know you've been watching that programme, and I thought it might help."

Sarah unfolded it and started to read. Felicia leaned over her shoulder so that she could read the flyer as well.

It was an advert for a local medium by the name of Harriet Swanson. It gave her phone number and described how she could communicate with those who had passed, in private sessions.

"Do you think I should?" asked Sarah.

"I think, if you want to, then I will happily drive you. Just don't tell your brother. Could be interesting, don't you think? She might just be a mad old lady, but she might give you the answers you need."

"Thanks, Dad. I'll think about it and let you know." Sarah had already thought about it. She would arrange to see this Harriet, but she wouldn't tell her father. He didn't really believe; he was just trying to be supportive. And she had no intention of talking to anyone about what had happened with the Ouija board with him in the room. He would

184

be furious at best, scared at worst. She knew that it had been a mistake, and she wasn't going to admit that to him.

Felicia was dead, but her female intuition wasn't. She saw the look on Sarah's face and realised what she was planning.

Chapter 23

Back at the mill, the ghosts still gathered. With everything that was happening, no one felt like doing anything fun, or even pleasant. Those who had family living in the area feared going home. With a hellion around, it wasn't worth the risk. Hellions are unpredictable by their very nature. Since the door was guarded day and night, there was the real risk that the hellion wouldn't go near it, and instead would find some other victim to torment.

Everyone was on edge. And it wasn't just because of the hellion. The door's influence stretched even to the mill. Once the ghosts left its vicinity, the effects lessened but were never fully gone. The fear and paranoia that emanated from it were potent and penetrated deeply into their souls. There was at least safety in numbers. For many, the scariest part was the long walk to and from the house. At least when they were at the house, they could face the thing that haunted them. At the mill, there was always someone there to watch your back. But travelling to and from the house, there were only two ghosts to keep each other safe from whatever lurked in the deepest recesses of their minds.

Now that there was a hellion in the area, the sensation increased tenfold. There was no doubt that they were being watched: the hellion would have been watching, even if the door wasn't. Hellions are all ghosts to start with. They do not sleep, they do not rest; they exist simply to inflict pain on others, so they can get the high they are so addicted to. The door was just a door, yet at the same time it was so much more – and it held back so much more.

"Luke has found a local medium. He gave Sarah a flyer with her details on. She said she would think about it, but I know she already has," Felicia said.

"You think she'll go by herself?" asked Tom.

"I do, so we'll have to find out when she's going so that at least one of us can go with her. William, you should go."

William nodded. He still had a sense of duty towards the family, even if all the dead were involved now.

"Claire could join me. You were able to use the Ouija board, so we know that you have the knack," said William.

"Of course I will, so long as Nat doesn't mind you taking me out," joked Claire.

That was settled. William and Claire would join Sarah at the medium's session. Hopefully this one would be more accurate than the Great Fundieni. This time they had two messages to get across: that her mother had not lingered, and that Sarah had to smudge the house properly.

Two days later, Sarah called Harriet and arranged to visit her house. It wasn't far from Sarah's school, so she would be able to walk there and back without her father knowing. From Sarah's perspective, the house was quiet. Her brother hadn't mentioned her sleepwalking again, and she had no intention of bringing it up. He thought that she was the one moving around, yet Sarah knew different. It had to be the man she had seen by her bed.

Sarah stood in front of her tall mirror. Carefully she cleaned the frame, then using another cloth she buffed the mirror until it was perfect. Her reflection was immaculate in the afternoon sun. Yet her expression wasn't. She had always loved this mirror; even when she was little, it had fascinated her. Her grandmother had left it to her in her will.

Normally whenever she looked into it, she remembered her wonderful grandmother, and her heart was filled with happy memories, but now it only showed her fearful expression. She had started to clean at the top and slowly worked her way down. As she sat to finish the lower half, fear gripped her. Her guts twisted with anticipation, her palms began to sweat, and her heart pounded.

She realised she wasn't alone. She looked all round the room. It was empty, but the feeling of being watched continued. It wasn't her brother and definitely wasn't her father, but someone was here, with her.

She looked into her own reflection. "Is there someone here? Mum, is that you?"

Nothing but silence.

"Can you give me a sign that you are here?" Nervously she looked around the room once more. But there was nothing. "Do you want to hurt me?" Still nothing.

Then there was a knock at the door.

"Are you decent? I wondered if you wanted anything from the supermarket," said her dad, popping his head around the door. Relief filled Sarah. It was nothing, just her imagination playing with her. It had to be.

"Why don't I come with you? I could do with a coffee," replied Sarah.

"Okay. Five minutes?"

"Yep. I'll be there in a sec." With that, Sarah shook off the feeling of being watched and left the house. She had been watching a lot of paranormal investigations; it must be her mind playing tricks on her. But if it wasn't, she would get answers soon. Harriet would be able to answer her questions. If she couldn't, then who could? The two words that the Ouija board had spelled out still plagued her. What was so dangerous? Or, rather, *who* was? Only a few days to wait, she kept telling herself, like a mantra.

Without thinking Sarah pushed the shopping trolley round, while her dad selected the items they needed. Her role was passive; all she had to do was to avoid running anyone over or knocking things off the shelves. Luke noticed her lack of interest and tried to engage her in the selection process, but soon gave up.

Having loaded the shopping into the car, they both walked round to the coffee shop for a much-needed break. It had been a while since they had talked properly. It was easier to talk without Oliver around, as most of their conversations involved him in some way. He was the one they worried about the most. To them he was still the baby, and always would be. Since the loss of their mother, Sarah's maternal instincts had kicked in. Her mother would – and should – have been there to protect him from the bullies and the bad dreams. She would have known how to guide him through such a difficult time.

But Sarah believed that her mother was watching them. But she couldn't discuss this with anyone. They would assume she had lost the plot. It was true that she had been through a great trauma, but she wasn't mad. Sarah was trying hard to find out the truth of the situation, while shielding the vulnerable from the horrors that it could expose.

"Are you sure you're alright? You seem to be miles away," her dad said.

"I'm fine. Just thinking, that's all. I've got so much work to do. It's madness, everyone's up to their eyeballs with stuff. And now Mr Harris has given me back my coursework with a load of corrections." Sarah breathed out deeply. She had all that on her plate and more, but the rest she couldn't talk to her dad about.

"Breathe. You'll get there. Just deal with what's in front of you, one thing at a time. You'll be fine. This year was always going to be manic. And I'm always here if you need me. Although we both know that I'm useless at science. But I'm willing and sort of able to help with other things."

"I know. I will be okay. Just a lot going on once. At least Oliver seems to be sorted."

"Has he said anything about those bloody bullies? He hasn't said anything to me, and I worry he feels he can't for whatever reason," said Luke.

"They've been sorted. I asked one of the rugby guys to talk to them; he got them to back off."

"He didn't hurt them, did he? You know I hate violence."

"He won't say. Just that he had words. So maybe he threatened them a little. In fairness, Dan is huge and scary, but he is just a big softie," replied Sarah.

"Well, let him know that I don't want anyone hurt. That never helps."

"I will." Sarah was lying through her teeth. The boys would have got what they deserved. They had taken pleasure out of making a bad situation worse. Karma, one way or another, would catch up with them.

"What do you think about that medium? Do you want to go and see her?" asked Luke.

"No, I don't think so. I've seen a few on TV and they all seem so fake. Better save the money and time."

"Are you sure? If you want to try, we can afford to."

"No, it's fine, Dad. Anyway, I think the subject of ghosts and stuff is interesting, but it's not real. Just a bit of fun." Unless they are standing by your bed at night, Sarah thought. With everything that she was withholding from her father, she was getting good at lying. But the lies were to protect him. White lies, not malicious or nasty, just a way to shield him from the truth.

Sarah knew that her father had been heartbroken after losing her mother. She had fought so hard and for so long against the cancer, yet it still won, robbing him of the love of his life. He might never be the same again. Sarah knew that her father was doing well, all things considered, but deep down he was lost. Their mother had looked after all of them, and now he was having to get used to doing things for himself. But it was the ache of loneliness that cut the deepest. When he thought no one was watching, he would let his mask slip. On more than one occasion Sarah had found him crying, either in their room or sobbing into the washing-up. He had the look of someone who was okay, yet deep down he was drowning. He didn't know what to do for the best, so he tried to do everything, over-compensating for being the only parent.

Sarah loved her dad with all her heart, but his constantly checking up on her was getting to her. But he couldn't see that he was making things worse for his baby girl.

Chapter 24

The day had arrived. William and Claire waited outside the school for Sarah. The moonlight wasn't very bright that day, but they could just about make out faces in the gloom. Sarah bid goodbye to her friends and turned left rather than right. Her friends seemed not to notice that she wasn't heading her usual way home. The two ghosts followed her for around half an hour before she stopped outside a very ordinary house – a basic three-bed house in the middle of a housing estate.

The garden was well maintained, but nothing unusual. There was no sign of garden gnomes or other weird ornaments in the garden. A simple, neat border lined the small driveway. It was full of blooming flowers and the faint hum of bees. The person that lived there might not be a medium, but they definitely had a green thumb. On the drive sat an average car – nothing that give a hint of the goings-on within. Sarah took out a slip of paper and read the address again, checking it against the house number on the front door. It matched, yet surely this couldn't be the house that she was looking for?

Sarah had stood on the pavement for too long, someone would notice her. She was just about to leave when the front door opened. In the doorway stood a small old woman. Smiling at Sarah, she beckoned her in.

"You must be Sarah. Come on in, my dear. I don't bite. I'm Harriet, in case you're wondering."

Sarah said nothing but smiled back at this seemingly harmless old lady. They walked down a narrow passage and into a small but perfectly formed dining room. Through a doorway on the other side, Sarah could see a kitchen, neat and spotless.

The dining room was warm, welcoming and cosy. In the middle was a round dining table with six chairs neatly placed around it. On the table was afternoon tea, set for two.

"It's been cold today, so I thought that you might need some tea. Please sit and make yourself at home, dear. There's no standing on ceremony in this house." Harriet poured out a cup for Sarah and handed it to her, then did the same for herself.

Harriet was a short woman. She was rounded in figure, cuddly rather than fat, with a close perm of silver hair. The wrinkles in her face showed the time that she had lived through, yet they complemented her eyes, making them shine even more. The twinkle in her eyes was brightest when she smiled, which seemed to be all the time.

"Why don't we start by you telling me why you think you need my help?" said Harriet.

"Okay." Sarah swallowed hard; she had dreaded this moment for weeks. She would have to tell her everything. "I lost my mother last year to cancer."

"Oh dear, I'm so sorry," said Harriet. She took Sarah's hand, holding it gently and with genuine compassion for her loss.

"I needed to talk to her just one more time. So I tried a Ouija board."

"Oh dear." Calmness and worry filled Harriet's formerly joyful face.

"I know it was my mother – she wrote out the words *danger* and *stop*. So I did, then I burned the paper and glass I had used. But…"

"But that's when things started happening?" continued Harriet.

"My brother says he has heard me sleepwalking, but I don't think it was me."

"Have you seen them?" asked Harriet as she took a sip of tea, still holding Sarah's hand.

"Yes. There was an old man next to my bed one night," said Sarah, starting to shake.

"Did he hurt you?"

"No. He just sort of stood there, looking at me, then he turned off the light. I freaked out!"

"You would do. Then what did he do?"

"I got a few messages. The first one was just before I tried to smudge. The second one I got a few days ago."

"You tried smudging, but it obviously didn't work. What were the messages, dear?" questioned Harriet gently.

"They were both written on mirrors. The first one told me to smudge, the second one said *demon*."

Silence filled the room.

William and Claire had followed Sarah into the house. William leaned against a large dresser, while Claire sat at the foot of the stairs that were in one corner.

"Who did that?" Panic was etched over William's face. He knew all the ghosts well by now; they all did. But he didn't know anyone who could write on mirrors. That was a very rare gift.

"No idea, but whoever it was, they're on our side! Could it have been Pa or Simon?" replied Claire.

"No – they would have said they could do that. It would have saved a lot of time and effort." William shrugged.

Sarah and Harriet were still silent. Sarah was trying to avoid eye contact with Harriet, so sat staring into her cup of tea. Both her hands were now free from the old lady's grip, and she carefully held the cup and saucer.

"Right. I think I know what is going on… When you use a Ouija board, even a home-made one, you open up a portal. It's a bit like a doorway between us and what comes next. But generally, they aren't good. Have you noticed any damp or mould suddenly appearing?"

"One of my walls is a little damp, but there's no mould."

"Right. It sounds like this man, whoever he is, is trying to tell you there is a demon. You said you smudged, but then you got the message about the demon?"

"Yes. I did my room – all the corners – with a blessing stick."

"When you smudge, you have to do the whole house, not just the room you did the summoning in. I doubt the man is the demon. Demons normally make themselves look like children, or something else non-threatening, not adult men. But you think the messages are from your mother?"

"Well, yes, who else would it be?" said Sarah.

"You would be surprised. When we talk about the paranormal, we might not just see or communicate with people we have known; we might also see people who have been connected to our house, or land, in the past. So, the man could be anyone."

"I suppose it is an old house. There are bits that date back to the sixteenth century, I think."

"So, the man you saw could be one of the old inhabitants. He might have been woken up by the Ouija board. If he didn't hurt you in any way, then he is probably just keeping an eye on things."

"I hope he's not watching everything I do. I don't like the idea of him watching me get dressed or showering."

"I doubt it. Normally spirits like that pop in and out for a few moments at a time. It doesn't mean your mum is there or isn't there, just that he is around. Finish your tea, dear. Then I will talk you through how to smudge the house properly, because it seems to me that that's what you need to do."

The session was supposed to last an hour, but by the time Harriet had finished telling Sarah exactly how to smudge, and the importance of doing it sooner rather than later, close to an hour and a half had passed. Sarah was keen to get going. She had lied to her father and her friends. She had told her father that she would be out with friends. She had told her friends she was going to see her grief counsellor. She didn't want any of them to catch her out and expose her lies.

Sarah reached into her bag and grabbed her purse.

"No dear. There's no charge for a cup of tea and some advice. Save it for yourself. But when you are done with the smudging and you feel up to it, come back and we'll see if we can find your mother. It's best done after you've got rid of any unwanted attachments. Your mum is unlikely to come through if there is a demon about."

Sarah began to walk towards the door, now very aware of how late it was. "Thank you so much – you really have helped. I will do the smudging and will let you know when I can come back."

On the long walk back to her house, Sarah thought about the man she had seen. Could he have been checking up on her? Was he really harmless? Or was Harriet just too nice, and assumed everyone else was? It would take her time to sort all this out in her head. Talking about it had helped a lot, but she still had a lot to work out.

William and Claire were also silent, trying to work out who had left messages on the mirror. How could they have missed a talent like that? If it wasn't someone they knew, who could it be? And how had they written the messages without anyone seeing them? The door was guarded day and night!

Communicating with Harriet would have to wait until after Sarah had smudged properly. Then, hopefully, they would be able to find out who was helping them.

Chapter 25

Sarah was finally home. So was William. Claire had gone back to the mill to fill them in on what they had found out. Hopefully someone there would know who had left the messages.

Sarah reached out and took hold of the door handle. She inhaled deeply, smiled to herself, then opened it. Inside, her father was busy cooking supper, while Oliver sat at the dining table doing homework.

"You alright? I thought you'd be out 'til later," said her dad.

Sarah put down her schoolbag and put the kettle on. "I'm fine. We only went for a quick coffee. Everything alright here?"

"Yes. We couldn't find Oliver's football boots, so we'll have to go and buy some more. Where did you go for coffee? We didn't see you."

Sarah had to think fast. "We went to that new place at the other end of the high street."

"Any good?"

"Expensive. I doubt we'll go back. But it was nice to try somewhere new. When do you plan on going shopping?"

"Probably Saturday. Maybe find some new trousers as well, we could both do with some. Do you want to come?"

"As much as I'd love to help you two shop for trousers, I think I'll pass."

"Too much fun for you?" Dad replied with a sarcastic smile.

"Definitely. How long 'til supper?"

"About twenty minutes."

"I've got to finish something for tomorrow. I'll be down in a bit."

Sarah was suddenly very pleased with herself. She had successfully covered up her meeting with Harriet, and if Dad and Oliver were going to be out Saturday, she would be able to smudge the whole house uninterrupted.

Upstairs, she opened her laptop. She would need a fresh blessing stick, and she'd have to order an express delivery if it was to get here in time. While she did that, William told Simon and Ethan all that had happened at Harriet's.

"None of us can do that!" exclaimed Ethan.

"Don't look at me. I can't do it," replied Simon.

"Whoever it was, they are helping us, that's all I need to know. The big question is, when will she do the smudging?" said William.

"Probably Saturday. Luke and Oliver were talking earlier about going out to the big shopping centre then," said Ethan.

Ethan leaned over Sarah's shoulder to see what she was doing. "She's ordering a new blessing stick. You'll need express delivery. That one there." He pointed at the screen, but Sarah couldn't hear him, or see the finger pointing to the express option.

"Saturday does seem like the most likely. Who should be here?" asked William.

"Hopefully none of us. As soon as she starts or looks like she is going to, we all have to leave the house and be outside the boundary. Anyone inside it will be banished for the rest of their deaths. Which isn't good – believe me, I know," said Simon. The pain of being banished from his own home still cut deeply. His pain was written all over his face.

"So hopefully only a few more days of guarding that thing," said Ethan as he looked up at the elephant in the room.

"We can but hope. Any sign of the hellion?" asked William.

"Nothing. He must have found someone else to pester," replied Simon.

"Poor buggers," said William. "I guess we will have to deal with him next."

"How?" asked Ethan. The single word expressed his frustration. Simon wouldn't tell them how. No one had the faintest idea why he refused to tell them. Was the solution that hard? Was the hellion that dangerous? Ethan wasn't the only one getting frustrated by Simon's lack of disclosure. All of these things were implied but were never said; they didn't need to be.

"One thing at a time. Let's get rid of that bloody door first," replied Simon.

With her order placed, Sarah closed the lid of the laptop and began to get changed. The three men saw her take off her shoes and jumper. Knowing what she was doing, and without saying anything to each other, they all left the room. Outside in the hall, William bid the other two goodbye. He wasn't on duty, so he left to go back to the mill.

Dawn was breaking for the dead. In the fresh light William walked slowly back towards the mill. Normally he would have walked with purpose, the need for sanctuary being the first and only thought in his mind. But today was different. The birds were singing, the air was sweet, and there was finally an end in sight. There was still the mystery of who had left those messages, but trying to work that out wasn't a priority right now. Whoever the writer was, they were helping, not hindering.

William walked slowly, taking in all the joys of this new dead day. The flowers were just starting to appear, and the hawthorn trees were in full blossom. It was a beautiful day, full of warmth and with a light breeze. This would be one of the last warm days the dead would have this year. As life returned to the world of the living, for the dead there was a slow descent into winter.

William loved spring. At this time of year, he was suitably dressed. During the depths of winter or the heights of summer, he wasn't. He had been buried in his best trousers and shirt, and the new shoes he had got from the cordwainer, finished off with his belt, pouch and the cross that his father had carved him around his neck. These were not for working in but were only worn for feast days and attending mass. Keeping up appearances was as important then as it is now, and his mother was very strict about when his best clothes could be worn.

With the weight seemingly lifted from his shoulders, he allowed himself to wander. Off the main road he walked down an alley he had only vaguely noticed before. Since he had returned, he had been caught up in other things and hadn't really had the chance to explore and rediscover the town. The alley opened out onto a smaller street that ran parallel to the high street. In William's time, the small market town had been a maze of alleys and small streets. Since then, the streets had been altered dramatically. For William this meant the town had lost a lot of its character and charm. Most of this seemed to have died as the town aged. Whereas once only one person had to walk down a road, now it needed to be wide enough for a car to pass. So, buildings had been lost and pathways and roads had widened and straightened in a bid to help drivers.

Instinct took over. William turned left, and to his amazement he found himself outside an ancient church. He had been baptised and buried here. Memories took over, too many to focus on. A lump formed in his throat. He knew the exact spot in which his remains had been placed, but he didn't dare go there, not yet.

He walked into the porch and through the door into the church proper. So much had changed since he was last here. In his day there hadn't been pews for people to sit on; you were only allowed a stick to lean on if you were elderly or infirm. He wandered up towards the altar, looking at the bare walls. Before the plaques naming some local family of importance had been put up, the walls had been painted with so much colour. The wall to the left of the altar depicted the soul's transition to heaven. In the centre was a skeletal man. Around him, all manner of forms were being tormented in purgatory. To the left of this was hell, complete with demons, fire, and vivid images of torture. To the right was heaven, with people and angels all smiling and bathed in a golden light. As a child the images of hell had held his gaze, yet as he learned its true meaning, he had begun to hope and pray that he would one day reach heaven, not hell.

The wall to the right of the altar depicted the life and great works of Jesus Christ. Nearest the altar was his birth, with wise men, angels and animals in attendance. William smiled to himself, remembering that one of the wise men was bending over to look at the baby. Unfortunately, these scenes hadn't been painted by da Vinci or any other great artist. William, his brother and their friends had joked that this wise man looked as if he was farting, given the looks of awe and wonder on the faces of the angels directly behind him.

Then on to the miracles Jesus had performed: the feeding of the five thousand, curing the blind and the sick. Then finally, nearest the entrance, his crucifixion was shown. A truly horrid scene, his mutilated body on the cross, with the crown of thorns, blood seemingly coming from everywhere. To one side stood his mourners, all showing deep grief. To the other side were those who had been crucified with him: an apparently unending vista of crosses with poor souls nailed to them.

Reaching the altar, he turned around and saw in his mind's eye the painting that had once covered the whole of the front wall, *The Resurrection of Christ*. It was golden and bright; hope beamed down onto all those who dared to look at it. Now the wall was barren. Whitewashed during the Puritan rule, now only a few wood and stone carved plaques could be seen. The church had been vandalised by those who didn't believe, and didn't appreciate what had once been here. The trauma was still so fresh and evident. It was such a shame. Had he been able to, he would have wept at this loss, and might never have stopped. He looked down in mourning for this bereavement. William turned again to face the altar, crossed himself and knelt down to pray.

When he had died, the church ruled everyday life – and death, for that matter. Daily life meant working hard as it does now, but back then you were expected to attend mass, or at least pray, each day. Fitting everything in when there was no reliable way to tell the time was difficult, but that was just the way things were.

Death during those times had been different as well. William had died young and unexpectedly; this had almost been shameful to those around him. He had never been on a pilgrimage, he had little to give away in terms of alms for the poor, and his family, although they were reasonably well off, couldn't pay for prayers to be read for him. At the time, people were taught that when you died your soul automatically went to purgatory, to be tormented there for a certain length of time. This time could be lessened if you had done great deeds such as a pilgrimage or if you had fought in the Holy Land. Giving alms to the poor or paying for prayers was expensive, but would also shorten your stay in this state. William had died suddenly, meaning he had had no time to confess his sins; the church taught that these sins would therefore remain with him, as they hadn't been forgiven.

When William died, he spent a great deal of time in this church praying for release from this purgatory. At first, he hoped it would end with his funeral, then he hoped that the prayers of his family and friends would end his torment. Eventually he gave up and resigned himself to this purgatory as something he just had to get through. Not all ghosts believe what William does; quite a few don't even believe in heaven or hell. They just believe in the next step, the next stage, in this crazy existence that we call life and death, whatever that may be.

At least his time in this state was interesting. He might not be able to do much, but he had gained a new family. He was engaged in daily death and he had a job to do – for now.

Chapter 26

William left the church without visiting his grave. He knew he and his family would be there. His father had made a cross with his name engraved on it, but time would have rotted that away long ago. He didn't need reminding of all that he had lost. He wanted to focus on the here and now: the family he had now still needed him, and he needed them.

Back at the mill, the ghosts were sitting in the field near the stream. On any other day this would have been a relaxed scene, but not now. The door was still there, the hellion was still on the loose, and there was still the mystery of who was helping them. William picked a spot next to Stan and they sat in the sun, soaking up its warmth and light.

Saturday came all too slowly. Everyone was nervous. Would Sarah smudge, and would it be successful? It was only a few days away, but to those watching the door, or those at the mill, it seemed like weeks. The last shift was taken by William and Nat. They watched in silence as Sarah prepared for the task. Downstairs Luke and Oliver left to go shopping; this was her cue to begin. Sarah waited a few minutes, watching out of the front room window. She was worried that her father and brother would return, but they didn't.

William and Nat stepped out into the light of the new moon. Outside the house waited all the ghosts, eager to see what would happen. Inside the house Sarah lit the blessing stick and started to smudge in the front room. The ghosts outside remained silent and still. The air was warm and thick with anticipation. Something was coming…

The ghosts huddled together, desperate to see what was happening. Only Simon and Pa had ever witnessed this before. For Simon, it was a painful reminder of the home he had lost; to everyone else it felt like hope, tangible and certain. As Sarah finished smudging the front room a wave of energy exploded from the house, knocking the ghosts to the ground. Sarah moved into the dining room, then the kitchen and the utility room. With each room smudged came another wave of energy, building in intensity, forcing the ghosts to step further and further away from the boundary of the house.

Sarah smudged the hallway and up the stairs, totally unaware of the ramifications of this simple ceremony. Again, a blast of energy belted out. The ghosts were gathered nearly halfway up the road by the time Sarah began to smudge the spare room. As they were unable to see her progress, the waves of energy came as more of a shock, but still they increased in force.

"Is anyone keeping count?" asked the master.

"I think we're up to seven," replied Pa.

"I thought it was six," said Tom.

"I don't know, but she must be nearly finished. How will we know when she's done?" asked Ethan.

"Trust me, we'll know," replied Simon, a glint in his eye.

Another wave of energy hit them hard. If the world of the living had been affected, the blast would surely have taken out windows, such was its strength. The ghosts remained totally focused on the house and the waves of energy coming from it. In the darkness, they were unable to see the sky that the living could see. With each blast the sky darkened and clouds built, heavy with rain.

Sarah had reached her parents' room; it was the last room but one. She started smudging, careful to smudge every corner and hidey-hole. The room filled with the smell of burning sage and other herbs. The smoke from the blessing stick was thick and white. Every few steps it wafted into her face, making her eyes sting. By the time she had finished the downstairs, her vision was impaired; standing in her parents' room, she felt almost blind. Sarah continued to say her prayers, bumping into things as she moved around the room.

She finished the room. Outside, the wave was enormous. Claire and Mark were near the top of the road, hoping that they were far enough away from the next blast, but they weren't. The pair were blown clean off their feet. For a brief moment, Mark flew through the air. Without anyone to catch him, he hit the ground as hard as the others. Luckily, he was dead, and somehow bounced into a neighbouring garden. Pa, in his bright red Santa suit, was thrown into a parked white van. He hit the side hard enough to set off the car alarm. As he flew through the air, his mind went into freefall, allowing this latent skill to come out. The rest were tossed far and wide. The master was the only one that managed to keep on his feet. He had done this by holding tightly to a gate post.

"Is that it?" asked Tom.

"Not quite. Should be one more to go, by my reckoning," replied Simon.

With that, all the spirits grabbed whatever they could. Mark and Claire took shelter behind a wall, while the others braced themselves for the big one. With heads bowed and grips so tight their knuckles were white, it came. But it wasn't what they were all expecting. A gust of wind blew past them, enough to rustle clothes and the odd leaf, but nothing more. Once it had passed, they could smell the sweet scent of flowers. It was strong, almost overpowering, then the heavens opened in a sudden cloudburst.

"It worked! Yes! You go, girl!" screamed Simon and he and Pa began to dance in the rain. Within seconds they were all soaked to the bone, but not one of them paused in their celebrations. It was over – Sarah had done it. And that was all that mattered. Rain fell hard for a good five minutes. Water flowed down the street in a great river towards the drains at the bottom. Meanwhile the dead cheered and danced and congratulated themselves in the deluge. Then, as quickly as it had begun, it was over. The moon was still visible, the clouds had clearly parted.

To the living this was just a downpour, but to the dead it was a sign that the smudging had indeed worked. William and Nat hugged, then with a pat on the back Nat said, "We had better go check."

"Claire, are you coming?" asked William. "I feel like it should be we three."

"I am." She pushed the wet hair from her face and took hold of Nat's hand, then William's. The three ghosts were no longer scared by this house, and so they marched confidently inside to see if the door was indeed gone. Outside Sarah's door, the three paused. A sudden anxiety gripped them.

"Ladies first," said William.

"I believe that's age before beauty," replied Claire, smiling warmly at William. He nodded in agreement then walked boldly into the room. Sarah was standing at the dresser. The half-burned blessing stick had been extinguished and was bobbing up and down in a glass of water. Behind her the door was gone; just bare wall stood in its place. Without thinking, William stepped towards it and ran his hand over it. The relief was almost too much. His head dropped and he leaned against the wall, trying to hold in his emotions. Nat recognised his friend's state and placed his hands on his shoulders, then kissed his head.

"It's over, mate. We survived. We all survived," Nat said in a shaky voice. William turned and faced his friends. Without saying a word, the three hugged. There was no need for words, not in this moment.

Sarah was unaware of what was happening or what she had done, but nevertheless she felt the relief that they all felt. She sat at the end of her bed and stared blankly into the quiet room, a smile on her face. She had no idea where it came from, but the feeling was strong and was here to stay.

After a few minutes the three spirits left the house, their fists raised in celebration.

"She bloody did it! It's gone!!" shouted William to the crowd of waiting ghosts outside. Cheers and hugs were again shared by all. Felicia kissed everyone on the cheek. Mark bounced from person to person, a huge smile across his face. The master's legs had gone when the shout went up. He sat on the pavement smiling, his head bowed with exhaustion; he was so pleased that the worst was over.

This feeling of joy remained for several days for all those present. With no more shifts to attend and with the threat gone, they all slowly headed towards the town. Tonight, they would party. The nightclub was the best place for that. All of them – the young, the old, new friends and old – worshipped at the feet of success.

Chapter 27

The spirits got to the club just as day was dawning for them. Inside the club, the staff were setting up ready for the busy Friday night. They sat in a quiet corner waiting for the revellers to arrive. They were able to relax for the first time in months. Conversation and a general feeling of victory made the time waiting fly by. Before they realised it, the club was packed and music and drink were in full flow.

The ghosts spent the night dancing and singing. Both living and dead revelled in the simple fact that they were here, surrounded by friends and family, and everything was good. For the dead gathered here, things weren't good; they were amazing.

The high of their collective relief kept them going all night. It's not normal to see the elderly in a nightclub, let alone trying to copy the latest dance moves. Stan had tried to twerk before, now he was an expert. He had clearly been practising on his own. Now he tried to teach others how to perform the manoeuvre. It took the master a few minutes, and then he, Stan, Pa, Simon, William and Nat lined up and began twerking for the others.

The night had been full of happiness and fun. When the club closed, the ghosts went their separate ways, and planned to meet up the following day back at the mill.

William felt great, yet he also felt the overwhelming urge to visit his family's graves. Outside the sun was shining, but with little warmth to it; winter for the dead was definitely on its way. He slowly made his way towards the church, a smile on his face and a spring in his step. This time he didn't go into the church itself; instead he headed around the building. At the rear was the graveyard.

This graveyard was old. It was full and no more burials happened here, but there was some space for urns to be buried after cremations. The headstones were a mixture of shapes and sizes, intermixed with the odd stone tomb. They were in varying states of decay, but on the whole the area was well maintained and pretty, for a graveyard. As William walked towards his own grave, he stopped to read the occasional epitaph. All around him the dawn chorus was starting, while the dead's sun began to set below the horizon.

He reached the area where he had been planted so many years before. At the time of his funeral this area had been full of wooden crosses. Now it was just grass. None of the markers had stood the test of time, apart from one headstone, which had been propped against the hedge. William didn't need to get close to it to see that it was so old that its engraving could no longer be read.

He knelt and placed his hand on the grass in the general area of his family plot. "I don't know if you can hear me, but I'm still here. The house is still there, and a lovely family lives there now – you'd like them. Things haven't been easy, but they will get better. I can feel that it's almost the end of the line for me, so I'll be with you all soon. I just wanted to come and say hello. I'm the only one here. I'm glad none of you lingered. You obviously led better lives than I did, but that's okay.

Purgatory isn't all that bad. I've made friends, some might as well be family. And we've had some adventures. You wouldn't believe what things are like now – it's so different to how they were. And yet they are still the same in so many ways. I love you all, and I miss you with all my heart. I'll see you soon." With that William stood up and wiped his dry eyes.

He slowly walked out of the graveyard, no longer looking at the headstones. He was gripped by loss. Grief never truly goes away; it just becomes easier to deal with. Even after all these centuries, William still missed the fun he'd had with his brother and the feeling of hugging his mother. He had hugged other mothers, but none of them gave the same reassurance that his mother's embrace did. Walking though the closed gates, William began to smile again. He missed his family, yet he had found the prefect replacements – for the time being, at least. He knew in his heart of hearts that his father,

223

mother and brother wouldn't take offence at this; instead they would be glad that William had such good people around him.

William's mind was a tangle of thoughts. There was overwhelming joy at getting rid of the door, mixed with fond memories of the night spent in the nightclub, tinged by thoughts of his long-lost family. Instinct took over and he walked, not with a purpose or destination in mind; he just needed to walk off the last twenty-four hours. After several hours, he wasn't sure how many, William found himself outside his home.

Inside he found the family sitting down to Sunday lunch, lovingly prepared by Luke, who was becoming a much better cook. The smell was intoxicating, and conjured up memories of Christmas with his own family. Yet there was another smell, rich and sweet, but also slightly bitter. It was the residue of the blessing stick. Sarah, unbeknown to William, had lied about her activities while they had been out. She had blamed the smell on a failed cooking experiment, which her dad had believed. Given his own steep learning curve in the kitchen, he could understand how these things happen.

The conversation was relaxed and calm, helped by a glass of wine for Luke and Sarah. But that wasn't the real cause, it was the blessing. The impact of the door's presence was huge; it wasn't just the ghosts that felt it, but also the living. To this family it had just been an uneasy feeling; dismissed as part of the grieving process, no doubt. But if only they knew the real reason they had felt that way.

After dinner, Sarah and Oliver washed and dried up. William sat in the front room with Luke. The two of them watched *Antiques Roadshow*. In between the valuations and insights into an item's history, they could hear the two teenagers laughing in the kitchen. Cleaning is normally a laborious task that has to be got through, but at times it is the best thing in the world. The casual conversations, laughing at a shared experience, or simply flicking bubbles at each other. It was clear that the whole house had breathed a huge sigh of relief now the door and its psychological impact was gone.

All too soon it was time to check that everyone had the right clothes and homework ready for the next day. Sarah ironed shirts for all three of them, and trousers for her brother and father. Her skirt didn't need it; after she had sat for a few minutes in it, it always looked like she had never bothered.

Slowly the house settled down to sleep. The TV and lights were turned off and the front and back doors locked. Luke was the last to go upstairs, but Sarah was the last to turn off her light and snuggle down into bed. It had been a while since she had seen the man standing by her bed. For a long time, she had thought about him every time she went to bed, fearful that he would come back. But that wasn't the case anymore; she was convinced that he was just checking up on her.

Sarah had done the Ouija board and opened up a portal. She knew that she had made a huge mistake, and that would never happen again. The thought of having someone checking in every so often wasn't that bad. No doubt if she did do anything stupid again, he, whoever he was, would be there to point her in the right direction. After all, it could have been him who had left the two messages for her. And if it hadn't been him, he must be okay. He hadn't hurt Sarah, and he must have met her mother.

Sarah's mother was a shadow of her former self when she died. Before the cancer, and the pain and visits to the hospital, she had been been in her prime. She was gentle and kind to her family, but if anyone was rash enough to threaten them then God help them, for she, like so many mothers, was fierce when required. She had her faults, but that was what made her an individual, and not just a carbon copy.

Sarah missed her so much. But for the first time in ages, she felt the stirrings of hope. She had done the smudging and got away with it. Now she would make an appointment to see Harriet again, and maybe this time she would take someone with her. She could take one of her friends – they all believed in the paranormal, but she wasn't sure which one to take. And she couldn't turn up with three mates in tow. If she took her father, he might say something to Oliver. Anyway, it might help him to move on with his life if he could talk to his lost love. She would have to think about it more carefully; sleep was the order of the day.

Sarah closed her eyes and drifted off into a peaceful sleep.

William checked the house and its inhabitants, then left for the meeting at the mill.

Chapter 28

At the mill some of the ghosts had already arrived by the time William got there. Those who were there were still buoyant and happy from the previous night. Things were starting to get back to normal. Discussions ranged from the door and Simon's unwillingness to share his knowledge, to the state of the various shops in town.

As the day progressed, spirits wandered in, talked a while about nothing in particular, then left. Things felt normal and almost dull, but William had a niggle in the back of his mind, but he couldn't quite put his finger on what was wrong. Instead he continued to laugh and talk with the others, sharing in these pointless, precious moments with his new-found family.

No one had seen the hellion since that day outside the house, so the general consensus was that it had had moved on to someone else, away from them – hopefully, very far away. Before too long the thin moon rose behind the clouds. It gave very little light, so the spirits that had remained at the mill settled down for the night.

When light returned to the world of the dead, William made his way back to the house. He knew that it was only a matter of time before Sarah arranged to see Harriet again. He would need to continue his vigil if he was to find out when. Over the next few days, William was able to see how family life was now. Things truly had settled. Sarah and Oliver were doing well in school, and Luke was coping with his new role. There was still the odd hiccup, but generally things were good.

Sure enough, Sarah rang Harriet and agreed to go and see her two days later, this time with her dad. She had spent a lot of time thinking about it and had come to the conclusion that he was the best person to take, providing he said nothing to Oliver. Luke was desperate to help his daughter deal with the loss of her mother, so he promised to keep it between them. William told Nat and Claire, and they decided that the three of them would go together. One way or another William had to get his message across to Sarah.

Then the day came. Luke and Sarah drove to Harriet's house. Oliver was staying at a friend's house, so he was oblivious to their plans. William, Claire and Nat squeezed into the back seat. Car journeys could be comfortable, but not always. After what seemed like hours they arrived at Harriet's house. Luke parked down the road because there was no space outside her house.

Sarah walked ahead of Luke and boldly rang the bell. Harriet answered the door with her traditional smile.

"Oh, my dear, you must be Sarah," Harriet said with a sly wink. "And this must be Dad. Please come in, we're in the dining room." Harriet took Sarah's hand and rushed them into the dining room. Behind Luke followed the three spirits, keen to see what Harriet would do.

The dining room was very different to the last time Sarah had joined Harriet for tea. The curtains were closed, the outside world banished from this sacred space. Candles flickered from all corners, and there was the pleasant smell of burning oils. Seated around the table were three other people: two young ladies and a middle-aged man.

As Sarah and Luke entered, they all shook hands and introduced themselves. Each of them had a drink. Not tea this time; wine was the order of the day.

"Do either of you want a drink before we get started?" asked Harriet.

"A glass of red would be nice. Sarah, what do you want?" replied Luke.

"I'll have the same, if you don't mind."

"Of course. You can give me a hand. Please take a seat, Luke." With that Harriet ushered Sarah into the kitchen, which lay behind the only other door in the room. In the kitchen Harriet took down two more glasses and poured wine into them. William followed them, keen to hear what they were saying to each other.

"So how did the smudging go?"

"Okay, I think. Nothing has happened since. So I guess it worked."

Harriet passed her a glass and started to make her way out of the room.

"Well, I hope you're going to make yourself known tonight. I guess you have a message. You must, or you wouldn't be here." She looked directly at William and smiled gently.

He was stunned. She could actually see him! This was amazing, not to mention unexpected. Silence hit William hard: he was frozen to the spot, unable to say anything.

Back in the dining room the living sat, while the ghosts stood around them. It was cramped, but not uncomfortable. The room felt full to the brim, yet there was still space to move around in.

"Right. How are we all doing?" Harriet smiled warmly at everyone. "Sarah and Luke are here to hopefully speak to Amber. These lovely people are here to help. Richard is learning how to master his natural talents, and Sophie and Ann are here for moral support. Richard, if you get anything don't be afraid to say, we're all open here. Are we all ready? Sophie, could you get the lights?"

The room was silent and still. Everyone closed their eyes. Luke looked round the table and realised that he should probably join in. Without opening their eyes, they all joined hands. Sarah took hold of her father's and Harriet's hands. Luke's other free hand was taken by Richard. It wasn't the most comfortable thing in the world to Luke, but for some reason he found it reassuring, even if Richard was a total stranger.

"I know you are here. Come forward and introduce yourself, please. No harm will come to you while you are in this space," Harriet said softly.

Claire stepped forward and spoke. "Hello, my name is Claire. I have a message for Sarah and Luke."

"Please focus all your energy. Only positive energy in this circle. Come closer."

Claire was now so close to Harriet that they were almost touching. "I'm Claire. I have a message for Sarah and Luke."

"I have someone – a young lady. Focus, my dear, I want to hear you."

"Try touching her – it worked with the Ouija board," suggested William.

Claire reached out her hand and placed it on Harriet's shoulder. "I'm Claire. Can you hear me?"

"I have a Claire here with us."

Luke opened his eyes. In the candlelight, he could see a lot of blank faces around the table. She was a fake, he thought. This was a cold reading, and it wasn't that good.

"Amber didn't linger, she moved on."

"Thank you, my dear. Claire is telling me that Amber has moved on. She couldn't stay with you, my dear," Harriet said, squeezing Sarah's hand gently. "Was it peaceful? Was she in pain?"

"Yes it was peaceful and pain-free. The portal is closed, and the demon will not come through."

"It was a peaceful passing, dear. I'm sorry, I know you wanted to speak to her. But she isn't stuck, and that's a good thing."

Sarah's eyes began to water. She had been so desperate to speak to her mum just one last time. Luke wasn't shocked by this. Harriet was a con artist, but at least this might put an end to the idea of communicating with Amber.

"Thank you, Claire, you've been most helpful. You can step back now."

Claire did as she was instructed as she was exhausted by the effort. Only once she had let the connection go did and sat down did she realise that she needed to mention the door and Sarah's need to properly smudge.

"Is there anyone else who would like to come forward?"

William edged his way round the table and chairs and placed a hand on Harriet's shoulder. "My name is William. The man that Sarah saw was a sort of guardian spirit."

"Richard, are you getting anything?" asked Harriet.

"No. I think that's all we're going to get tonight," he replied.

"Please, if there is someone there, please use all of our energy and step forward." Harriet closed her eyes and concentrated.

"My name is William. Can you hear me now?" he said, placing both hands on Harriet's shoulders.

She shook her head. "Nothing. They've gone. It's like that sometimes. I'm sorry."

Everyone let go of their neighbour's hands and opened their eyes. It had only been a few minutes, but they all felt stiff, and their eyes were gritty from staring at the inside of their eyelids.

"Who the hell is Claire?" said Sarah, as she looked at her father.

"No idea. I think your mum had a relative called Claire, but that's going back a long way. We tried, that's the best we can do. I'm sorry. Are you alright? You're not too disappointed?"

"No, I'm fine. It would have been nice to speak to Mum. I'll be okay, really, Dad," replied Sarah. She picked up her glass and took a large swig of wine.

Everyone else was calm and talking about how successful it had been. Sarah didn't share in their enthusiasm.

"Why can't I do anything? I'm older than both of you combined. What's wrong with me?" William shouted. Anger boiled in him. His lack of ability frustrated him so much. He took a swipe at a candle. To his surprise, it moved and fell to the floor, spilling hot wax over the immaculate carpet.

"Well, we know someone's here," said Richard. No one living had been near the candle. He closed his eyes. "Can you speak to us, spirit?"

"Go on, you have to try!" insisted Nat.

Normally William would have taken care to avoid walking through the living, but in this instance he didn't care. There were too many people in the way. He stood behind Richard and put his hands on his shoulders.

"My name is William. The man Sarah saw was a guardian spirit. The demon and portal have gone."

"Please give us a sign that you are with us," Richard said.

William closed his eyes and concentrated hard. "My name is William," he said slowly and calmly.

"I give you permission to use all of my energy."

"I AM WILLIAM." His teeth clenched in anger. His temper was starting to get the better of him.

"Nothing, I think they've gone. Sorry." Richard sighed.

"Or maybe that was Claire?" replied Harriet.

William's temper flared once more, and he kicked the sideboard hard. BANG. The room fell silent. Again no one had been near the sideboard.

"Ow, shit, fuck, bollocks! That really hurt! Don't look at me like that. I know I shouldn't have lost it, but I couldn't help it," said William, as he hobbled towards his friends.

"I take it that hurt?" said Nat sarcastically.

"Please can you give us another sign?" asked Harriet.

"No way. Once was enough!" replied William.

"Well, at least they noticed you. I might as well not be here," said Nat.

"I'm glad you're here. If you weren't, I wouldn't be able to laugh at William," said Claire, before bursting into laughter.

"Who needs enemies when I have you?" said William, then kissed Claire on the forehead. He was smiling, but his foot still hurt, and would continue to throb for the next few days – a painful but important reminder that he shouldn't lose his temper, regardless of the situation.

Over the next few days Sarah and her father talked about their experiences at Harriet's house. Luke was convinced that she had been a fraud, but Sarah seemed to think otherwise. She showed little interest in the paranormal after that night. Which was probably for the best; she had her exams to focus on.

The weeks turned into months. William checked in with the family on a regular basis, but he never saw anything to worry about. The family was finally moving on, and living with their grief. Stress over exams and daily life replaced tearful moments hidden from view.

Harriet might not have provided the means to talk to Amber, but she had provided closure.

Chapter 29

The hellion's breath was as toxic as his words. "Just do it. Kill yourself. No one will miss you. He won't, she won't. Do it, then all of this will be over."

The poor man he was tormenting wasn't in his home, as you might expect; he was homeless. Although this meant the hellion had fewer objects to move or doors to slam, he could still pour venom into the man's already troubled mind.

In life, the hellion had been the apple of his mother's eye. His name was Peter Maxwell, and he had worked in a high-street shop. Out of work, he was obsessed with his car, which would ultimately lead to his death.

He had gone through a red light, then had been chased by the police. During the high-speed pursuit, he had taken a bend too fast. The car left the road, flipped and hit a tree. Peter died on impact. His girlfriend, who had been in the passenger seat, escaped with only a few broken bones.

Peter had started with her.

In life their relationship had seemed perfect. But behind closed doors, she had been his punching bag. Fearful of his response, she had never summoned up the courage to tell anyone. Peter was always careful to hit her where no one would see. There was always a reason for his violence; she was clumsy, she made him angry. Then he would claim that he hadn't meant it, or that it would never happen again. But nothing ever changed.

When Peter found himself stuck, he continued to take out his frustrations on this vulnerable woman. He quickly learned to speak to her in her sleep, but his weren't the kind words of a loving partner. Peter did to his girlfriend what he was now doing to this wretched man. Thankfully she had friends who recognised the signs of him haunting her. Peter's girlfriend was given a full spiritual cleansing and moved elsewhere, away from her memories.

When Peter realised he couldn't get to his girlfriend anymore, he found someone else to torment. Such was his addiction to the negative emotions, he never thought about his ex. All he could focus on was his next fix, and his next victim.

The man in question was called John Harper. He had been a soldier who had served his country with pride and dignity. He was kind and thoughtful to his family and friends, and there was nothing that he couldn't deal with. Then came active service.

He fought in the desert against the last of the Taliban. Desperate to keep hold of their territory, they committed horrors too haunting to speak of. It was these acts that led to John's downfall.

First, he was discharged on medical grounds from the army. He was lost without his comrades and the job he loved so much. Civilian life didn't suit him. Then he was diagnosed with PTSD. Treatment hadn't helped with his nightmares or anxiety. Unable to hold down a job or support his family, he lost his house. Temporary accommodation made things a hundred times worse. Now he – this once strong man – was broken into a million pieces.

He had walked out of the bedsit in a daze. Unsure where he was or what he was doing, he carried on walking. He didn't stop for several days, by which time he was well and truly lost, both physically and mentally.

He had been living on the streets for several months by the time the hellion found him. He was easy prey for such a wicked soul.

*

After the removal of the door, Tom and Ethan had returned to their beloved shop. The two of them spent their days watching the living buy and upgrade phones. Business was business, after all. They were out of place in their butchers' outfits, but they couldn't change their appearance, and no one had ever noticed their presence. As far as they were concerned, they were helping.

From the main window they could see all they wanted to see. To the left was a small grocer's shop, to the right was a smart solicitor's office. Opposite stood the shop and its owner that caused them so much frustration. It was the bakery. The owner was a kind young lady. Even though her shop had only been open for a relatively short period of time, it had a steady stream of customers. In the town, her popularity rose sharply when people realised what she was doing with her leftovers. Each night before she closed the shop, she would give away anything that was going stale to anyone that asked for it, in particular, the homeless. Those with money would offer a donation, those without didn't. It was a fair system that stopped bread going to waste.

Over the last few years, the rate of homelessness in the country had risen dramatically, and even this small town had a few. The church opened up its heart to them and did its best to help them out of the situation, offering them rooms in parishioners' own homes, and hot lunches free of charge. But for every person they got off the streets, there were two more to take their place.

Neither of the butchers had been religious while they were alive. To many they were seen as stingy, but even they could appreciate the merits of giving away slightly stale bread. What they objected to were the homeless in the first place. They believed they brought the area down, by begging or just by looking dirty. Tom and Ethan also believed that helping locals who ended up in that situation, this would encourage others from further afield to come into the town and use people's hospitality for their own ends. When the issue had first appeared, they had voiced their opinions at a meeting. The ghosts around them felt the need to hammer home just how selfish and nasty they were for thinking such things. And we all know what happens to spirits who are so hateful...

It was a wet Tuesday afternoon when Tom and Ethan first noticed John. He was standing near the front door of the bakery. He was a familiar face around town. He never begged; instead he would offer to help people carry bags to their car. Normally they would offer him a few pounds for being so helpful. Out of all of the homeless people who had been through the town, he was the one that Tom and Ethan liked the best. This time John wasn't alone, which was unusual.

Tom stared at the two men through the glass door. Even at this distance he could see something was wrong. "Back in a minute, just gotta check something," he said, as he walked out into the rain.

"This one's mine, go find your own!" shouted the hellion as Tom approached them.

"What do you mean 'he's yours'?" Tom asked, using his fingers as quotation marks.

"Look, if you want a hit, go find another waster. This one's mine, I've done all the work. So fuck off."

Tom was already annoyed and scared. This had to be the hellion that William and Felicia had seen. Leaving a hellion to burn themselves out was the normal thing to do. But Tom had a knot in his stomach that told him something was truly wrong.

Tom had died just before the end of the Second World War, so he had come across hellions before. Instinct screamed at him that this was a different beast. The hellion leaned towards John. "You're nothing, you're useless. No one will miss you."

"What the hell are you doing to him?" Tom was getting angrier with every second that passed.

"Look, old man, if you want a hit then you have to soften them up. All I'm doing is telling him what he already knows. You can get a nice steady stream off one of these guys if you're careful."

"And if you're not?"

"Then they kill themselves. Then you get a massive hit! It's great, but then you have to start on a new one."

"You do realise how sick and twisted you are? How can you do this to another person?"

"He's homeless for a reason. This is all they're good for." He smiled and breathed in deeply. Closing his eyes, he absorbed the fear and self-loathing that was coming off John in waves. "Now piss off, I'm busy."

Ethan had followed Tom across the road, eager to find out what was so interesting.

"He's the hellion," said Ethan, pointing at him. His hand shook with fear at the mere sight of this thing. "What's he doing to John?"

"I think we had better go." Tom's voice dropped to a whisper as he took Ethan back to the shop. "We'll deal with him later. Simon knows how. Just leave him be."

"And don't come back – go find the sausage or something!" the hellion shouted as they went back to the safety of the phone shop.

"The sun's nearly up. We can go to the mill and get help with this one," said Tom.

Until the rising of the dead's sun, they stood guard, watching the hellion and his victim from behind the window. Tom and Ethan soon knew where John would have gone; he was a person of habit. As soon as the dead sun rose, Tom and Ethan headed to the mill. Their only hope was that Simon was still in town, and that he was able to do what he had claimed he could do.

The mill was empty. Unusually, Tom and Ethan were the only spirits there.

"We had better go and find him. That little prick doesn't care if he drives John to kill himself," said Tom.

"No, he will be here. Or someone else will know where he is. We have to wait. John's strong, he can cope," said Ethan, crossing his fingers behind his back.

"You're right. Better to get the solution in the next few hours than run around all night trying to find him. Someone will come. They have to," replied Tom.

Tom and Ethan waited nervously for someone to arrive with the answers they needed. After what seemed like an age, William, Claire and Nat arrived, quickly followed by Stan, Pa and Simon.

"We've found the hellion, and he's trying to kill John – you know, the homeless guy," said Tom.

"What? That can't be right. Hellions like to stay in people's homes. There's more stuff to throw at them there," replied Claire.

"This one's whispering all sorts of nasty things to him. He doesn't care if he drives John to suicide!"

"What do we do, Simon? We can't let this happen," said Nat.

"We need Felicia and Mark. Does anyone know where they are?" said Simon.

"She might be in her old house," said Stan. "It's just down the road from mine."

"I'll come with you. Do we know where John is now?" asked William. Ethan and Tom nodded.

"You and Stan go and get Felicia and Mark; we'll find where John has bedded down for the night. Then we'll all meet up at the phone shop," suggested Ethan. Everyone agreed and then left to perform their allotted tasks.

William and Stan walked quickly towards Stan's house. Felicia's old house was just up the road. As they passed Stan's house, William could see Stan's wife sitting in the front room. She was watching the TV, a microwave meal for one on her lap.

"How's she been since you passed?" asked William as they moved on towards Felicia's house.

"She is definitely doing better. She always had lots of friends, and of course she has the children and grandchildren to keep her company. It's rare that she stays in! But at least she's happy. The last few years, the only places we went together was the hospital. And that's no life for her."

"Do you think she will … move on fully?" William had to ask. He had only seen her for a split second, but she looked healthy and happy. And if she was doing so well, it could just be a matter of time before she found herself another man. Probably not the love of her life, but someone she could talk to and who would care for her.

"I don't know. I just hope she finds someone less ill than I was. She deserves someone nice. And I don't want her to be lonely," replied Stan. Changing the subject, he said, "Felicia's house is just up here on the left." A few minutes later they arrived at a lovely Victorian house. From the outside, it looked far larger than the standard houses around it. The windows on the ground floor were bay; on the second floor the windows were large sash ones. Through the windows they couldn't see either Felicia or Mark, so they headed inside.

Stan called out, "Knock, knock. Felicia, are you home?" as they entered the property; both of them had unconsciously wiped their feet as they came through the front door. It wasn't needed, but it was still good manners.

"We're upstairs. Come on up," Felicia shouted down to them. William followed Stan up the stairs. On the landing they found Felicia pondering a wall covered in tester paint. The current owners had selected several shades of red and one shade of brown.

"Hello, boys. Which one do you think for the stairs? I like this one," said Felicia.

"Um, I think that will be too dark, but yes, that one would look alright," replied William.

"We need you and Mark. Tom and Ethan have found the hellion. He's driving John – you know

John, the one who's homeless, not the one in the supermarket – out of his mind," said Stan.

"From what Tom and Ethan told us, this hellion doesn't care if he drives him to suicide. Simon and the others have gone to find them. He said we need you and Mark, but he wouldn't say why. Will you come?" continued William.

"Of course we will. Where are we meeting them?" replied Felicia as she walked into the room behind her. On the floor, engrossed in wallpaper samples, was Mark. As soon as his name was mentioned, he began to crawl towards the group on the landing. Felicia gathered him up in her arms and turned to the two ghosts behind her.

"The phone shop," said Stan. "Are you up for this, little man?"

Mark smiled at Stan and began to bounce in Felicia's arms. He was clearly excited.

The five spirits arrived at the phone shop a short time later. Simon, Pa, Ethan and Tom were already inside, waiting for them to arrive. The rain was still pouring, and even though ghosts can't get ill or even cold, there's still little point in standing in the rain.

"You made good time," said Ethan as they walked into the closed shop.

"Where are the others?" William asked.

"Trying to convince the hellion that he doesn't need to do what he is doing," replied Tom. "It won't work, he's completely addicted, and he doesn't give two shits about anyone but himself."

"How can we help?" Felicia asked Simon. Simon stepped forward and took hold of Mark, who had since down.

"I'm afraid the only one of us who can do anything is you," Simon said, looking into Mark's eyes. All around him the ghosts stood looking confused and silent.

"What do you mean?" asked Felicia as she stroked Mark's head.

"Only a pure, innocent soul can destroy a hellion. But it's not without risk…There's a good chance that Mark will burn up with him."

"You can't. I won't let you!" objected Felicia, grabbing Mark from Simon's grasp.

"Why don't we ask Mark?" suggested Simon. The others knew that Mark was clever for a baby, but did he really have the ability to understand the full ramifications of this suggestion? Simon took Mark once more and placed him gently on the ground. Then he and Felicia stepped back, away from him. "If you do this, you would be saving a life. But it could kill you. If you want to try and help poor John, crawl towards me. If you don't, crawl to Felicia. No one will be angry if you choose not to. It has to be your decision."

Mark sat down and looked hard at his feet. Then he got on all fours and began to crawl towards Felicia. When he reached her, he pulled himself up to standing. She bent down to pick him up, but before she could lift him, he kissed her on her cheek. He then turned away and crawled over to Simon. He raised his arms, so that Simon could pick him up. He had made his decision. Felicia started to sob silently, her hands clasped over her mouth to silence her fear and dismay.

"If you can do this, you will go down in history!" said Pa, a broad smile on his face.

"What does he have to do?" asked William.

"All he has to do is touch him. A hug would be best, but a simple touch should do it. As soon as he starts to burn up, we will get you away from him. Okay?"

Mark smiled in response.

"I'll put you down near the hellion. You will have to crawl to him. That way, you can change your mind whenever you like." Mark continued to smile at Simon, but it wasn't his normal broad smile. It was somehow stunted.

Mournfully the spirits walked around the corner. They followed Tom and Ethan to where John and the hellion had settled for the night. John was sitting under the shelter of the covered walk. Water ran down the centre, where it was open to the elements, but it was dry at each side. The doorway to the chemist's shop offered the best shelter.

Here, out of the rain and the wind, was John, sitting on his sleeping bag, a few bags of possessions around him. He looked tired. How much more could he take?

Around him stood the hellion, Claire and Nat, arguing.

"You can't do this. He's a human being!" cried Claire.

"He is mine. He isn't good for anything else. Why do you think the government wants him here? They want them to die, and if it helps us, then that's a good thing. I'm not doing anything wrong," argued the hellion.

"But you don't have to do this. Please, there are other ways to survive. We can show you," said Nat.

"What do you mean, join one of your mothers' meetings? No thanks. I need this, not your pathetic existence. I'm doing a public service," said the hellion. He turned from them and sat down next to John. "No one can save you. Just kill yourself," he whispered into his ear. John turned towards the hellion. He could clearly hear him, but it was unclear if he could see him. His gaze was firmly fixed in the direction of the hellion, but his eyes were watering so badly that it was difficult to tell for sure.

The others approached from around the corner.

"Well, will he be turned?" asked Pa.

"No. He really doesn't care about anyone but himself," replied Nat.

"Looks like you're up, little man. You can change your mind whenever you like," Simon said to Mark as he lowered him to the ground.

"Oh, you've got help. I'm so scared. Piss off, the lot of you! You can't stop me," shouted the hellion.

Mark began to crawl towards him. He had purpose and was surprisingly quick.

"Is this the best you can do – a baby? What happens if I kick it into next week?"

Mark didn't slow down, even with this threat. The hellion was now standing, poised to kick Mark if he got any closer. Felicia was terrified for her ward. Nat and Simon were holding her back, preventing her from interfering. Mark looked at the hellion, and the hellion looked back at him. Suddenly the hellion seemed to realise that the baby was the one he should be scared of. Self-preservation hit the hellion hard. He took a step forward and kicked out, but his leg passed straight through Mark. Mark was still approaching steadily. The hellion backed off fast. Before he realised it, his back was against the wall, and he was unable to escape.

Mark stopped just short of him. He looked back at the others and smiled, then leaned in for the kill. Mark was still on all fours. He stretched out a hand and made contact with the hellion. At first he grasped his trouser leg then, leaning further in, he touched the hellion's leg. The hellion started to shake; electric shocks ran throughout his body. Pa saw that it was starting. With surprising speed and dexterity, he flew at the two of them, grabbing Mark in mid-flight and rolling away from the hellion, his arms wrapped around Mark for protection.

The hellion's shaking was getting more pronounced. Then it fell to the ground and began to convulse. Pa, who was inherently protective of children, carried Mark back to the others. They all watched as the hellion began to writhe in agony. Cracks began to appear on the hellion's skin, through which light could be seen. Then the hellion burst into flames. His screams were incomprehensible. The flames licked higher, then with a sudden blast the hellion was gone. All that remained was ash, which slowly drifted down onto the wet ground.

This ash was soon washed away by the heavy rain and wind. The collection of spirits stood there, astounded by what they had witnessed. Simon looked around, but he couldn't see John. He had seen the hellion burn up. Fear of what he was seeing had driven him into the storm, without his things, and with considerable speed. Silence descended. Then Mark cheered loudly, his arms raised in celebration. Everyone's gaze shifted from the remains of the hellion to Mark, who was bouncing in Pa's arms. Pa lifted Mark onto his shoulders and bounced with him. Soon everyone was smiling and dancing in the rain, while Mark beamed and gave high fives to them.

Chapter 30

No one, not even Felicia, knew how Mark had died. He had woken up in this state, on the ground. With no one around, he started to crawl. Felicia had been walking along the high street one day when she had seen him crawling down the road. Not on the pavement but in the road, traffic passing through his body without affecting him. Deep down, Mark wanted to know what had happened to him and why he had been abandoned, but for now he was happy with his 'mum', Felicia.

Felicia's past life came back to her without thinking; her time as a nanny was the happiest part of her life. Now in death she had another baby to love and protect. Without a moment's hesitation she had scooped him up, away from the traffic and his lonely life.

Mark and Felicia soon developed a system of yes/no responses to questions. After an hour or so Felicia had established that his name was Mark, and that he had been alone and crawling for some time.

But he was unclear how long this had been the case.

Yet here he was, a tiny baby and hero to all of those around him. Unlike other children, he hadn't turned nasty or become a hellion. Most dead children rebel, unable to accept their new existence or the absence of familiar loved ones. In the majority of cases, they stay with their parents and get more and more upset at their inability to communicate with them. This inevitably leads to violence and hatred and other hellion-like behaviour. Mark, by contrast, was truly a pure soul, capable of more than anyone could imagine. Thanks to Felicia's kind heart, Mark had been saved from such a horrible fate.

John had been saved. Not only was the hellion gone, and he was free of this torture, but John had seen the hellion burn up. He had run as far and as fast as he could. Fear of what he had seen had kept him going, despite his legs turning to lead and his heart beating so fast that he felt it would burst out of his chest. With legs like jelly, he had run out in front of a police car as it cruised around the town. The two policemen got him into the car, thinking he was drunk. But after hearing his description of the hellion and what had happened, they concluded that he was mad.

A few days later John was sectioned. For most people, this is a bad thing, but for him it was the first step back to his life. His wife was found; she and the children were able to visit and to tell him all the things he needed to hear. Soon the toxins from the hellion were out of his system and he was able to look forward to a better life with his family around him. Despite this, he never forgot what he had witnessed, but he did stop talking about it.

John wasn't the only one who was starting to heal. With the door and the hellion gone, all the spirits were recovering. They had quickly settled into a more relaxed routine. Every Tuesday William, Felicia, Mark, Pa and a few others would meet at the park, then go to the mill for the proper meeting. On Friday or Saturday nights they would all go to the club. The rest of the week was theirs to do with as they wanted.

Claire and Nat were usually conspicuous by their absence. William and Simon would wander the town, reminiscing about days gone by. Felicia and Mark were deeply engrossed in the renovations being done to their house. He might never have lived there, but after all the time he'd spent here, it was his house too. Meanwhile the master returned to the manor house. He liked to keep an eye on how his family was doing.

As the dead winter descended, the living wore less and less due to the heat of the sun. That afternoon William, Mark, Felicia, Pa and Simon met at the park. Dead snow fell on the sunbathers, who were out in force. Around the corner was the local veterinary practice. Those animals that had breathed their last at the vet's eventually made their way to the park. Mark sat in the grass with a couple of friendly cats, while the other ghosts sat on an empty bench watching a group of dead dogs play.

"How's Sarah doing these days?" asked Felicia.

"Settled for now. Oliver has decided they need a dog. Luke and Sarah are looking at rescues, but Oliver has his heart set on a puppy," replied William. "How's the house coming along?"

"They've started on the kitchen. You have to come and see what they've done in the bedrooms. They look amazing! Not sure what they will do with the bathroom… But they seem to have good taste," replied Felicia.

"Haven't seen much of the master, have you?" asked Simon.

"Oh, I saw him the other day, he's fine. The youngest is starting their GCSEs next term, so he wants to stay close to them. You know what he's like," said Pa.

The conversation came to a halt as four very excited dogs ran through them, knocking Pa off the bench. Lying on his back, he was set upon by the dogs, all of them keen to lick his face and to jump on him. Needless to say, they were soon giggling. Within the blink of an eye the dogs had realised that all the ghosts were their friends. Felicia found herself with a large German shepherd nuzzling her face, his huge paws in her lap so she couldn't move. William's lap was taken over by a small pug who just wanted to lie down and rest after all its running around. Meanwhile Simon helped Pa out from under a very loving but heavy Rottweiler and a smaller, but no less enthusiastic, mongrel. Simon and Pa laughed and winced under the exuberant dogs. Mark sat further away with the cats. One hissed as the dogs ran past, but they quickly settled back down to the matter in hand – belly rubs!

The afternoon passed with surprising ease. The cats were the first to fade. They had positioned themselves around Mark, snuggled down, their feet tucked underneath them. Their purrs got louder as they slowly faded away to nothing. Mark didn't move until the sound of the cats had disappeared. The dogs had spent some time getting attention from their new-found friends, then they began to run around, chasing each other. Happy and having the time of their lives, the group began to fade as one. They slowly evaporated from view until there was nothing left. These creatures had gone the way all ghosts want to go: happy and free of the cares of this world, ready, willing and able to find out what comes next. This was not the violent, painful burning up that the hellion had experienced; it was peaceful. It was a tonic for everyone, animal and human alike. The humans hoped that the end to their time here would be peaceful too.

The sun was still high in the sky over the living. For the dead, the moonlight illuminated the world, but even the moon was starting to set below the horizon. The group of spirits slowly left the park and headed to the mill. They arrived just as the dead sun was dawning. Around them there was a thick layer of ghostly snow, almost see-through yet tangible and cold to them. This ghost snow gave everything a halo of white, like smoke or thick fog, yet it clung to the tops of trees and bushes as well as to the ground.

The conversation was relaxed at the mill. They had discussed the distemper outbreak that had led to so many dogs being at the park; the current weather – both the heatwave that the living were faced with and the heavy falls of ghost snow; the renovations to Felicia and Mark's house; and how the living were getting on with their lives.

Several hours had passed when the master arrived. To say he was beaming would be an understatement; he was positively glowing.

"You won't believe what I've just found out!" he bellowed.

"What?" responded Pa, who had already caught this man's contagious smile.

"*Mostly Ghostly* is coming to the manor house!"

Shock and elation filled all the ghosts.

"Are you sure?" asked Felicia.

"Yes, the family have just finished talking about it. They're as excited as I am. I can't wait!" said the master, bouncing up and down like an excited child.

"That's amazing!" shouted William.

"We need to spread the word. Simon, Pa, will you go back to the city and invite everyone? This will be a party none of us will want to miss!" said the master.

"Of course we will. How far do you want this to spread? I can think of loads of locals that will want to come," said Simon.

"The more the merrier. Come one, come all, as far as I'm concerned. We are going to need all hands on deck if we're to give them a night to remember," replied the master.

"We'll need time to get ourselves together. Work out who can do what, that sort of thing," said William.

"Yes. You're right, so shall we all meet up here a week before?" said the master.

Nods of agreement and broad smiles came from them all. They had a few weeks to get the word out. Pa, Simon, Nat and Claire would leave for the city the next day, once they had been told the good news. Felicia, Mark and William would head to the next village, while Ethan and Tom would hunt around the local haunts.

They spent the next few hours plotting how they could make a real impact on the paranormal investigators. All sorts of suggestions were made, and a few ruled out. Things that had been ruled out included Pa showing himself; no one wanted to hurt the team, so thrown objects had to be done by those who could actually aim, and no one knew how to make a bad smell. What got everyone excited was the thought of using the fancy equipment that the investigators would no doubt bring with them. All the spirits had learned about electronic voice recorders and the like while watching the show, but no one had used them. It would be a steep learning curve for many.

When dawn broke on a new day the ghosts left, eager to get to their appointed destinations. William, Felicia and Mark walked out of town and down the road towards the neighbouring market town. William had been there twice when he was alive and twice after he had died; once when he was leaving, then again on his way back home. The snow had stopped, and had been replaced with persistent rain. It didn't bother any of the ghosts that much, but it dampened their high spirits. It took around five hours for the three to get to the market town of Newholm. It was quite different to their own home town. The town was contained within the bend of the river that ran around two-thirds of the town. It had retained a lot of its old buildings and small alleyways. It was smaller and lacked a lot of the shops that their town had, but it was still quaint and welcoming.

The first time William had been here was with his father and brother. They had come to the midsummer fayre. Like today, there were plenty of people milling around the town, with even more things to see and learn about, but the boys were distracted by the main event. A holm was an island or floating platform on the river. It was on this that fights were performed. On that day, two of the local knights had to fight, they both desired the same high-born beauty. Neither of them was prepared to back down, so it was decided that they would fight to the death on the holm. Luckily for the knights, it was a solid island on the west side of the town. They paraded through the town on their horses, dressed in shining armour and carrying their shields, which had their crests delicately painted on them.

William couldn't remember their names, but the sight of them as they came down the main road had left a lasting impression on him. William had to sit on his father's shoulders to see the fight. His brother, who was taller than him by this point, even though he was younger, stood on a barrel. The fight lasted an epic two hours. By the end, both knights were exhausted and bloody, then one caught the other off guard and delivered the killer blow. The sword pierced his throat. Blood flowed dramatically out onto the sand that made up most of the holm. William had always remembered the cheer that went up from the crowd on the banks when the duel was at last finished. Back then it didn't matter who the soon-to-be wife had chosen; these things were normally arranged by the father, and the young woman's father was happy for a knight to marry his only daughter. It would mean a rise in the social hierarchy that operated at that time.

By all accounts the couple were happy, but you can never really know what's going on behind closed doors. As William recounted these events, he could vaguely remember that the couple had at least three sons; the first was named after the loser of the battle. This was an unusual tribute, but knights were more like blood brothers, even when they were on opposing sides. In the major battles of the day, knights weren't killed, unlike the average soldiers. Instead they were taken hostage and then ransomed back to their family. Normally there wasn't even the need for restraints, or even guards. Escaping or running away went against the code by which knights lived. To do that would have brought great shame on them and their family; they could even be stripped of their knighthood, should they be so unchivalrous.

William told this story as the three walked slowly down the main road. Periodically they would stop to look at something in one of the many souvenir shops. They had become tourists, whether they wanted to be or not. Soon they came to the town square. Like so many market towns in the area, it had a black and white building on stilts to one side. The black oak and the whitewashed wattle and daub stood out proudly even after all these years. It was Wednesday: market day for the town. Around the square was a multitude of small stalls selling everything from cleaning products, fresh meat and vegetables to clothes and teddies. Felicia, Mark and William had nowhere to go; this was where the locals had their meetings. So they spent the afternoon looking through the stalls, examining their wares.

Mark spent an age looking at all the toys that were spread out over one stall and the pavement in front. He was fascinated by the movement sensors on one of the small dogs. If he waved his hands enough, the toy would bark or stand up on its back legs. Having got a response, he would giggle with excitement. The stall owner was convinced that this toy was faulty, as it kept going off when no one was there. His response was to reduce the price stamped on it. This made one small living child very happy, as she was able to buy it with her remaining pocket money. Mark's smile when the girl took the toy was wide, and he was clearly happy for her. He then moved on to another toy. The stall holder wasn't happy with these seemingly broken toys. After he had marked them all down, they were soon bought by happy customers. Mark then moved on to the other stalls to see what else he could find.

All too soon the market had been packed away. Products and people had gone, and calm and relative quiet returned to the area. The three ghosts settled themselves down on a nearby bench. They sat and waited for the locals to come for the night's meeting. After an hour the dead sun was up but with little heat, the rain had stopped and there was still a chill in the air. The dead can feel these changes, but they never feel overly hot or cold.

Soon enough, ghosts appeared for the meeting. First to arrive was Martin, a stern, tall man dressed in a sharp suit and hat. Without being told of his past occupation, the three spirits knew that he had been an undertaker – from his manner as well as the top hat he held under his arm. He was very polite, with a dry wit. Next came two old men, Bill and Alan. Both smiled from ear to ear when they realised that new people had arrived. The icing on the cake for them was Mark, who they quickly scooped up for a cuddle. Finally came a young lady called Elle. She was thin, almost gaunt, but beautiful. As they would find out later, she had died of cancer, but, unlike Amber, she had lingered.

"Is this everyone?" William asked Alan, who was waiting for his turn to hold the baby.

"Yes, there's only a few of us here."

William cleared his throat and stood up so that everyone could see him. "The reason we are here is because we have an invitation for you all. The TV show *Mostly Ghostly* is coming to the manor house in Bechford. They will be here in three weeks' time. The master of the manor house would like you all to join us for their investigation."

All the ghosts looked happy.

"Are you planning on giving them a night to remember?" asked Alan.

"Yes – but of course, with no ill will. We want to have fun, as well as give them something in return. It should be great fun. The master wants us all to meet up at the old mill about a week before so we can establish what we can all do," said William.

"You can count me in!" replied Elle.

"Me too," said Alan.

"And me – should be fun. We haven't had the chance to do anything like that for ages," said Bill while he continued to bounce Mark on his knee.

"What about you?" Felicia asked Martin.

"I'm not sure it's my sort of thing. Can I think about it?"

"Of course. We're not planning on meeting up until the 23rd, that's just over a fortnight away."

William, Felicia and Mark stayed for the next few days with these spirits. They were given a VIP tour of the town. They visited all the places of interest, and finally they visited the local haunted house.

"So, is this it?" said William.

"Yep. It's the council offices now, but it was the workhouse back in the day," replied Martin.

"It's a beautiful building. Shall we go in?" asked Felicia.

"I wouldn't recommend that. We used to meet here, but it was taken over a few years ago by some less than pleasant spirits. We avoid them and they leave us alone," replied Martin.

"At last count there were three hellions in there, but we don't know for certain. We don't come down here that often," said Elle.

The building was grand indeed. It had large windows and brick walls, and the main entrance was carved white stone. But since it was on a main road, dirt had built up to turn the stone a sludgy grey rather than the bright white that lay underneath. Through the windows on the ground floor, they could see into a neat modern office, worlds away from its original purpose. The ghosts felt that the building gave off a sense of foreboding that made them feel very uncomfortable. William and Felicia knew this feeling well; it was like the feeling given off by the door.

"Let's move on. Felicia, you will love this next house. It was built in the late eighteenth century by a local merchant. It has a stunning interior," said Martin. As they walked away, William looked back at this imposing building. The living weren't at work, but there was a lone face in one of the top windows. The woman was thin, with bags under her eyes and wild messy hair. She was there one second and gone the next. William continued with the others, fearful that this hellion might follow them. Luckily this brief glimpse was all they saw of the monsters that had taken over this establishment.

William and Felicia both noted the advantages to the dead of being in this town rather than back home in Bechford. With a sizeable river so close, none of them felt tired. No matter where they went in the town, the river remained a constant companion, providing all the ghosts with a steady supply of energy.

After a few days of getting to know the town of Newholm and its inhabitants, William, Felicia and Mark led Bill, Elle and Alan home to Bechford. The heat of the living sun was getting hotter by the day. A weather report said that the country was going to be bathed in sunshine for the next few weeks at least. There had been a discussion about whether or not they should use the bus, but given the smell of sweaty people that wafted off the bus when it arrived, the consensus was that they were better off walking. Anyway, they had the time.

The group of ghosts walked at a relaxed pace along the small road that connected the two towns. Even in the dark they could see all that they needed to. Unfortunately, with no pavement they were forced to walk in the road. The traffic was sporadic, so when a vehicle did pass them, they would instinctively move into the side, but the drivers never noticed these acts of courtesy.

In the hedgerows they passed all manner of songbirds and insects, all keen to raise the next generation, despite the unyielding heat. The journey to Newholm had been damp and more like an unpleasant march, whereas the walk back to Bechford was more akin to a winter walk with family and friends. In between the relaxed conversations they listened to the sound of birds singing and bees buzzing around them. William had left all thoughts of the council offices and the horde of hellions behind. Now the fresh air lifted his mind, body and soul.

Chapter 31

The next few weeks in the town were manic, to say the least. Nowhere was safe. The ghosts spent all their time trying to learn new skills or brushing up on techniques that they already had. Simon took a group down to the pub, where they all practised trying to be heard walking up and down the bar area. Felicia took another group to the day centre; there they all tried to make things move. Cheers and celebrations bounced around the room after someone had successfully moved some knitting or some other piece of crafting equipment.

The butchers, who had mastered the art of blowing things, took their group on a tour of the town's shops. They were careful to spend only a few hours in each shop, blowing at pieces of paper or flour in the bakery. Meanwhile the master held his advanced classes at the manor house. Everyone was expected to attend at least one, but most went to more than a few.

In between all this, the ghosts met and regained their strength at the mill. Swapping tricks and tips was all that mattered. William had no idea what he was doing, or where he was supposed to be. With all the chaos in and around the town, he had headed home. Felicia was taking her own classes, so Mark had joined William.

To William's surprise, Sarah had got there ahead of him. He sat on her bedroom floor with Mark, while Sarah lay on the bed checking Facebook. After a few posts about Earth Hour and the latest political scandal, she came across one from the fan page for *Mostly Ghostly*. It proudly announced their intention to investigate the manor house just outside Bechford. Sarah read the post carefully, then read it again. Her face lit up when she realised what this meant. In seconds she was racing out of her door and downstairs, yelling the good news to her brother and father. William quickly picked up Mark and followed her into the kitchen. The two of them stood smiling at each other while she bounced around the kitchen with excitement. The date was marked clearly on the calendar – even Oliver was keen. Luke, who had seen the candle move and had heard a loud bang come from the sideboard at Harriet's house, was still sceptical about the supernatural, but even he was smiling. Even if it was all smoke and mirrors, a major TV show was going to be coming to their small town. That was big news!

It wasn't just Luke who felt like this; all over the town, people had heard about the show. Shoppers who were normally too busy to stop and chat now stood for long periods of time talking about all the paranormal activity that they had noticed, much of it in the last few weeks. To the staunch sceptics, it was obvious that people had heard about the show coming and were blaming ghosts for normal, easily explained everyday occurrences that they had witnessed. It's true that a draught could be the reason why things kept moving in the newsagent's, but if you had been there and seen the selection of ghosts trying to ruffle the magazines and papers, you would know the truth.

All too soon, the day came. Outside the manor house the ghosts lined up to watch the arrival of the TV crew. Standing as the staff would have done back in the day, they remained still and quiet except for the occasional giggle or curtsey. But they did not wear the neat uniforms you would have seen on *Downton Abbey*. With two butchers, a man in a Santa suit, a Victorian nanny and baby, a fireman in his best uniform and an old-school rocker, they were an odd mix and truly a sight to be seen!

Ghosts had come from far and wide. They were all keen to show off to the new guests, but they were under strict instructions to let them finish setting up first. Instead they watched curiously as the team wired up the house. Cameras were put in most of the rooms; sensors were placed on the stairs; and trigger objects were placed around the house. Excitement exuded from all quarters. Soon the living sun would set and the investigation would start.

"Hello, and welcome to this week's episode of Mostly Ghostly. We are here at the manor house in Bechford! And it's fair to say we have all the support that we could hope for!" Jonas made the introductions from outside the house. The camera spun away from him and focused on a vast crowd of locals all cheering and shouting for the show's stars. Swiftly the camera moved back to focus on Jonas. "Join us as we investigate the manor house!"

The camera and cameraman then moved past Jonas and in through the impressive front doors.

"And cut!" shouted Mitch.

"Thank you all so much for being here. You will all be on the show!" Jonas turned from the crowd to face the team. "Right, let's switch to night vision and get the lights off. Let's do this!"

The team was made up of four men: Jonas, Mitch, Phil and Ian. Jonas was the main presenter, handsome and tall, wearing his worn brown leather jacket as always. Mitch was shorter, bald and covered in tattoos. Despite his appearance he was a big softie, self-schooled in the occult and the paranormal; there was nothing he couldn't explain.

Ian and Phil were the technical experts. Both had degrees in film production: Phil's was in video, whereas Ian's speciality was sound. He had the best hearing of them all, and did all of the EVP analysis. Both were of average height and build. The only major difference between them was that Phil wore glasses, but he still managed to walk into things on a regular basis.

The living sun was well down. Inside the ghosts could all see clearly by the dead daylight that streamed in through the windows. To the living, it was pitch black and foreboding, full of dark corners and blind doorways through which anything could leap out at them.

"Right, we all know what to do, so let's start on the walk-through," instructed Jonas.

With the lights off and their hand-held night vision cameras, they began moving from room to room, calling out. The first room they entered was the massive lounge. Unbeknown to the team of investigators, it didn't just contain large sumptuous sofas, but also several ghosts, all keen to take part.

John had travelled from the city to be here, and it was he who would get things started. In life he had been a firefighter. John had been buried in his formal uniform, even though he was retired when he died. His skill, and the only thing that he had mastered, was to cough so the living could hear him. He couldn't speak and be heard, but this didn't matter; a cough at just the right time was enough to get his opinion across.

"Hello, is there anyone here? We're calling out to the ghosts of this beautiful house. Can you give us a sign that you are here?" asked Jonas.

"We don't mean any of you any harm. You can use all of our energies. Please, we just want to know that you are here," continued Mitch.

John stepped forward and coughed loudly.

"Who was that?" asked Phil.

"Not me," said Jonas.

"Or me," said Ian.

"I've got you on camera, Jonas, and it wasn't me either," said Mitch.

When the dead make a noise that can be heard by the living, it has a slight echo. John inhaled deeply and coughed for a second time, this time even louder.

"Please tell me you got that?" said Jonas.

"We are all on camera. That was loud!"

"Thank you. That was amazing! Can you do it again?" said Jonas.

John coughed again, louder still. This cough could clearly be heard by the living – luckily the coughing fit that followed wasn't heard.

"This is brilliant. Who has the spirit box?" asked Jonas.

"Got it," replied Phil, taking a small speaker system out of his pocket. It was the spirit box. He switched it on and white noise filled the room.

Rapidly it switched from channel to channel, giving a constant flow of pure white noise.

"Right, everyone, concentrate and do what feels natural. Remember, we want to focus on the word 'welcome'," instructed the master. None of them had used one of these devices before, so they knew it would be a bit hit-and-miss to begin with.

"Can you see the thing in my hands? You can talk to us through it. Please try," said Phil.

"Is Bob with us? We know that's what the owners call you," said Jonas. Earlier that day, while Phil and Ian wired the house up, Jonas and Mitch had conducted several interviews with the house's owners and other people connected to the house. The master watched with a mixture of pride and pleasure as they recounted their interactions with him. Needless to say, Adam didn't reveal the tickling incident to the camera. Off-camera and away from the team he told his mother, who laughed. "Yep, that's our Bob alright!"

Jonas looked straight at the camera pointed at him. "As you will have seen from the interviews, this house has one ghost that many people have seen. Well, I say people, but what I mean is that he has only been seen by the children who have lived here. He has never harmed them, but I don't like the idea of him focusing on just the children. That, to me, says we could be dealing with a possible demonic entity."

"Demons love the energy given off by kids, and kids, let's face it, are gullible, and will believe that he is friendly when he might not be," continued Mitch.

"How dare he! He's a guest in this house!" exclaimed Felicia.

"He's probably spicing things up for the fans. Let him think I'm a demon. I'll get my revenge," replied the master, a twinkle in his eye.

"How?" asked Felicia. The other ghosts in the room were all concentrating hard on the spirit box, while Felicia and the master stood back and watched.

"I'll let William tickle them to death, or at least until they wet themselves," said the master, smiling from ear to ear. White noise continued to echo around the room, then at last the deep and unmistakable voice came through loud and clear. It was the master's.

"Demon. Revenge. Death."

Everyone, living and dead, stopped dead in their tracks. The master was nowhere near the group, but that was definitely his voice. But no one could understand why just those words had been caught on the spirit box. He had said those three words, true, but along with many others, and in a totally different context.

"Demon. Revenge. Death. This investigation just got a lot more exciting. We need to be on our toes tonight!" said Jonas, his hands shaking.

"That was a warning. Who do you want to hurt?" asked Mitch.

Felicia stood agog, looking at the master. He looked shocked, as if he had no clue what had happened. His voice had never been heard, and he hadn't been concentrating on the spirit box.

The gathered ghosts all rushed to congratulate him on this stunning victory.

"Nothing. Now, that could mean that they don't want to hurt us, or it could mean that they don't want us to know who they want to hurt," said Phil.

The team continued to ask questions for a good twenty minutes or so. The master was in no shape to respond. He had to sit down. The shock of being heard by the living for the first time in hundreds of years was too much for him. If there weren't so many ghosts around him, he would have let himself cry – at least, as much as any ghost could. Instead he held in his emotions and sat quietly, trying not to focus on his own success, but planning his next move. The ghosts were disappointed that they couldn't be heard, but they were all ecstatic that the master had been.

With no other voices coming through the spirit box, the team turned it off and moved into the next room: the grand dining room. A massive table stretched out before them. At a push, twenty-six people could be seated around it. The owners had set the table with their best china and glasses. Even in the darkness, it was an impressive sight. Normally the family only used one end, with the rest of the table free to be used for whatever was required – everything from making uniforms, sorting paperwork and the occasional jigsaw. It was a useful table, but tonight it was ready for a banquet.

The team entered the room and quickly made their way towards the far end. There, two pieces of paper had been placed, a large cross on one and a Bible on the other. A circle had been drawn around the pieces of paper and a camera, fixed so it couldn't easily be moved, was placed where it could film the paper clearly. Surrounding this end of the table were several ghosts.

"How are you doing in here?" shouted the master from the other end of the vast table.

"I think we have a little movement. It might take some time, but we will get there," replied Ethan. Over the past few weeks, he had learned to move things. Only very small things and only very slightly, but for him it was a new and exciting skill. Ethan, Simon, Stan, Chloe and an older lady from the city were tasked with moving these objects. In all likelihood, it would take them all night, but the master had every confidence in them.

The team carefully looked at the trigger objects by torchlight, making sure that they didn't touch them or the camera. The lights they were using weren't up to the task. The cross had been moved slightly, but the team could not see this subtle movement without the help of the main lights. They quickly moved on to the next room, the library.

The library was on the south side of the house. Every wall was covered with shelves of books. In the centre of the room was a selection of sofas and chairs, all comfortable and positioned perfectly. In between them was a series of lights: two on small side tables, the third a pretty Tiffany-style standard lamp. These had all been moved to the side of the room to allow a large table and chairs to be placed in the room.

On the table were a ball and a voice recorder. The family had long believed that there were others in the house and, since no one had seen them, all they could go on was what they had heard. In this room they had heard the sound of laughter on a number of occasions: to the untrained ear, it was the laughter of a child. In reality it was the master, who had read most of the books in the library, but he loved the ones that made him laugh. Being able to take a book off the shelf, turn the pages and read it gave him something to do when the house was silent and still.

The task of those in this room was twofold: to move something, either the ball or a book, and to be heard on the voice recorder, but laughing, not talking. The ghosts assembled included Claire, Nat, Tom, Mark and Martin.

"Here we are in the library. Isn't it a wonderful room? In here the sound of children laughing has been heard on a regular basis. So, we have a ball for them to play with and an EVP recorder, and hopefully we will get something," Jonas said. He turned from the camera and looked into the empty room. "We know that you're here. We brought you a ball to play with – we just want you to be happy. You can play with the ball if you like. Please don't be afraid, we won't hurt you."

"We've so got this," said Nat as he stroked Mark's head. Mark had been placed on the table so that he could try to move the ball. The others would also try, but as it was meant for a child, he got first dibs. The team stayed for a further twenty minutes or so, periodically calling out to the child spirit or spirits of the house. But they got no direct response.

"Right, we've just tried to laugh. The master has been heard laughing in here on occasion.. So… what do you call a ghost that haunts fireplaces?" said Martin.

"No idea," replied Tom.

"A toasty ghosty!"

There was a giggle from the spirits around him.

"What should the living say to a ghost when they meet?"

Shocked faces surrounded him; no one could have expected that he, of all men, had a sense of humour like this.

"How do you boo?"

The smiles got bigger.

"How do ghosts fly?" asked Nat.

"I don't know," replied Martin, chuckling to himself.

"British Scareways!" said Nat. Everyone broke into laughter. It was bad, but also good.

The spiritual jokes continued. With each bad joke told, the laughter got louder. The feeling in the room was of fun and mischief. Soon everyone, apart from Mark, was telling their own ghostly jokes. Needless to say, no one was going to leave this room unless they were forced to; they were having too much fun.

The investigating team had no luck in the library. The ball hadn't moved, and despite sitting in the dark just listening, there were no sounds of children to be heard. At least, not with their ears. After the night was done and they had time to analysis the tape, they would hear the sound of laughter coming from the library. They, like others before them, would believe that this laughter was that of a child. It's true that Mark was laughing and giggling with the others, but it wasn't just him that they heard.

Next on the team's route around the house was the cellars. "These cellars would have been a hive of activity when the house had staff. But now they are just used for storage. But they are amazingly well preserved." Jonas reached out and opened the door to the old kitchen. Only he and Ian had been down here before.

"Wow!" said Mitch. "This is amazing, it's all still here."

"I know, it just needs a clean and it could still work fine. It's like they just left," replied Phil.

"Jonas, you with us?" asked Mitch.

"Yep. This is just brilliant. I love it." He had been examining the old stove, which was more rust than metal, but even so, it was still beautiful. In the dim light of their torches, it looked to be in better condition than it actually was.

"Right. Shall we?"

Nods of agreement came from the rest of the team.

"Over the last few years the owners have heard all sorts of noises coming from down here, everything from shouting to footsteps. So we are just going to sit and listen quietly. We know that there is nobody else in the house, so any noises we catch are not down to human contamination."

"If only they knew just how full the house was at the moment," commented Pa.

"They might not be quite so confident," replied William, smiling. "Okay, people, it's time, let's make some noise!"

With that, all the ghosts began to walk up and down, with their own brand of silly walks. Elle was by far the best at this in practice, but today the pressure got to her and she was unable to make a single step heard. After a few minutes of trying and failing, her legs felt heavy and sore from all the stomping up and down. Elle stood back and watched as the others continued trying. In this room there were limited places to sit and rest, so she sat on one of the countertops. Exhaustion was setting in fast; the anticipation meant that she, like many of the others, had been too excited to rest properly in the days leading up to tonight.

As Elle allowed her body to relax, she leaned against a box that was behind her. Soon the hypnotic sound of the others walking up and down lulled her into a stupor. *BANG*. The box behind her had suddenly, and quite unexpectedly, shifted and fallen onto the floor. Everyone jumped.

William had been walking past the exact spot; the box had narrowly missed him, causing him to scream in a very girly fashion.

"Who did that?" asked Jonas, his voice shaking with fear.

"None of us, we're all over here," replied Phil.

"We'll have to look over the footage, but I think I got it," said Ian.

"Brilliant. Well, we wanted activity and we got it. Do you think that we should change tack and try the spirit box?" asked Jonas.

"Yep, sounds good, but I will need to change the batteries in about thirty minutes or so," said Phil as he took the machine out of his pocket. With a flick of a switch, white noise filled the room. Upstairs the sound had seemed quieter; down here in the confines of the old kitchen, it was deafening.

"Can you please talk into this device? We will be able to hear you if you concentrate," said Jonas as he pointed to the spirit box. The team huddled closer to it so that they could hear even the slightest noise. The white noise bounced off the walls and seemed to hit them even harder when it returned. Ian had his ear up close to the speaker when a sudden deafening scream came through. It took everyone off guard.

"That was a woman – did you hear that?" exclaimed Jonas, a mixture of fear and excitement in his voice.

"That was amazing! Can you do that again?" said Mitch.

"That was you!" Bill smiled and playfully patted William on the back.

"No, it wasn't, my scream was not that high-pitched. Maybe it's distorted?" said William.

"No, that is what you sounded like. Sorry mate, but that was not a manly scream." Pa giggled as he held his stomach. He was, like the others, trying with all of his might not to laugh. It wasn't working, so he walked away laughing quietly to himself. From the other side of the door the ghosts could hear his belly laugh. William was embarrassed, but at least he had been heard; that was all that mattered.

Above the bombardment of white noise, they all suddenly heard Pa's laugh coming through the speaker. To a child at Christmas it was a jolly sound, but in the darkness of the abandoned kitchen it did sound evil. The team once again froze to the spot. No one had expected that, of all things, to come through.

"That was a demon and no mistake!" said Jonas. The silence from the rest of the crew confirmed this idea. They didn't like it, but they believed they were dealing with a nasty spirit. Elle rushed to tell Pa. As she passed through the door, she found him sitting on the floor, still giggling to himself.

"You're a demon, apparently…"

"What?" replied Pa, wiping his face and trying to straighten up.

"They heard you laugh, and they shit themselves. If only they knew," said Elle.

"Maybe I should really blow their minds and show myself to them?"

"I think that might be a bit much for them right now. You'd send them running to the nut house." Elle giggled as she joined Pa on the floor. Pa put his arm around her and the two laughed together at the madness they had helped to create.

From upstairs, a siren sounded. The sound was so loud and high-pitched that it took everyone by surprise. The door to the kitchen swung open and the team raced through it and back up into the house proper. All the spirits quickly followed.

"What the hell is that?" shouted Elle as William helped her off the floor.

"No idea. Let's find out!" William shouted back at her.

In the main entrance stood the team, along with all the ghosts in the house. The sensors on the stairs were the source of the commotion. Suddenly the torchlight hit the culprit. Laughter erupted once more as everyone saw a cat sitting in front of the sensor. Unlike the cat that lived at William's house, this cat was pure white and as deaf as a post. He casually washed himself, oblivious to the chaos he had caused. Only when Phil leaned past him to switch off the sensor did the cat become aware that people were watching him carry out his personal ablutions. The cat slowly lowered his back leg and sat upright and meowed loudly, then began walking towards the kitchen and his food bowl.

The team's nerves were frayed, to say the least. So they decided to take a break. Phil followed the cat with his torch, guiding him to the desired destination. The cat paced back and forth, twining between his legs. Phil fed the cat then returned to the others in the parlour. The team sat in front of the monitors, still stunned by all the activity they had experienced. Phil poured coffee for each of them as they sat and tried to work out what to do next.

The dead stayed in the main hallway. With the sensors turned off for the night, several sat on the stairs as the master organised them for the next round. This would be the big push. They would pull out all the stops; there was nothing holding them back. Bouts of laughter and giggles spread through the group as they talked about what had happened so far. This was the best night that many of them had had in years – of either life or death.

Chapter 32

After an hour or so, the investigation team had composed themselves and refuelled both their equipment and themselves. Ready to face whatever the house could throw at them, they made their way back to the living room. Waiting for them were William, Nat, Simon, Felicia and the master.

"Are you ready for this?" asked the master.

"I hope so, are you sure?" replied William.

"Yes, they can take it. And they have called both me and Pa demons. Let them have it!"

The team were blissfully unaware of the ghosts watching them, as they set up another voice recorder and fiddled with the settings on one of the hand-held cameras.

"Are we all ready? Good. We know that you're here, and we want to help you. Can you knock once for yes and twice for no? Do you want us to help you move on?" Jonas asked, as he stood in the dark of the living night.

Behind Mitch, Felicia tried to bang on the door, but she wasn't heard. Across the room Nat stood staring at the side of a bookshelf. Deliberately winding himself up, he bounced from foot to foot like a boxer. Then he punched the bookcase twice, once with his left hand, then with his right.

BANG, BANG echoed out into the room. The note was low and hollow, yet quite quiet.

"Ow, that really hurt!" said Nat, cradling his knuckles.

"You did it, boy! Well done," shouted the master.

"Yeah, I did it. Good job I'm dead or I would have broken something. Someone else can answer the next question," Nat said flatly, as he walked slowly away from the bookcase, flexing his sore fingers.

"You should never punch with a closed fist. It's always a bad idea," said Felicia, taking his hands in hers and rubbing them gently. Nat winced with the pain, but the love and compassion that the two shared made up for it. He leaned forward and kissed Felicia on the cheek. "I'll be fine, thank you."

"That was two for no. Why don't they want us to help them? Do you like being here?" Ian asked the apparently empty room.

Nat looked at William, who stood by one of the sofas. William nodded and took a deep breath, then kicked the side of the sofa. *BANG*.

The team waited for a second bang, but there was just the one.

"I guess they like it here. Do you like hurting people?" asked Jonas.

Next to him William hobbled off. He had been heard, but the price was a throbbing foot. He limped towards Nat, who consoled his friend with a gentle rub on his back. They had done their part, for now.

Felicia squared up to the door. Clenching her teeth, she slapped the wood twice. The sound of two gentle but clear thuds was heard by the team.

"Okay. So, they like it here, but they don't want to hurt anyone. So… do you want us to get rid of the demon? We know there is one here. And we would be happy to do that for you," Phil said.

Simon tapped Felicia on the shoulder. She stepped back from the door and he stepped forward. He composed himself then hit the door hard. Two swift blows from his right hand echoed through the room.

"I really hope this is a short conversation," exclaimed Simon as tried to soothe his painful knuckles.

Felicia began nursing Simon's hand with hers. "What did I just say about punching with a closed fist? Muppet." She smiled sweetly at him. Simon took her hand and kissed it gently.

"Sorry, Mum. It won't happen again. Or at least until it's stopped hurting!" Simon continued to hold Felicia's hand.

"How many of you are there?" asked Jonas.

William playfully slapped the master on the back.

"Good luck answering that one," he said as he smiled at the master. The master cracked his knuckles and moved to be right next to the team, who were together, away from where the bangs had been heard. With no solid objects nearby, the ghosts all waited to see how the master would get the required number of bangs across to the team.

The master stood up tall and straight, then began to stamp on the floorboards. With both feet he soon reached double digits, but then his legs buckled under him and he fell back into an obliging chair behind him.

"I got twelve," said Jonas.

"I thought it was fourteen," said Phil.

"Pass. I stopped counting at six. Regardless, it was a lot," said Mitch.

"Either way, the owners that there might be one or two, but if that isn't a wind-up, this place is full to the brim!" said Ian. In the darkness only the night vision cameras could detect the shock that was written all over his face.

"Are there nasty spirits here?" questioned Jonas. "Or are you just trying to scare us?"

All around the room, the assembled ghosts were done. Each had injured themselves in order to get the right answers across. They would not be knocking out any more responses tonight.

The team continued to ask questions, but soon even they realised that they weren't going to get any more answers. So eventually they left and moved on to the next room. Buoyed by the activity they had heard, they couldn't wait to see what evidence they would get next.

In the library, the group of ghosts had told all the jokes they could think of. There was only one thing left to do – tickle someone, but who would play the victim? While this was debated, Mark continued with his task. He had been placed back on the table. Pa remained by his side, trying to encourage him. Mark was small and quiet, yet he was rapidly becoming the stuff of legend. This was his task and he wasn't going to fail.

In his long death he had moved things before – flowers, mainly, that wasn't the only thing. The others didn't know how he managed to pick flowers, but from his perspective it was simple. He focused on the love he felt for that person, then reached out his hand to collect a token of his affection.

The ball was different. He had tried to concentrate on the love he felt for those around him, but that hadn't worked. Now he relaxed into almost a lotus stance, but his short, stumpy legs didn't bend that much. He closed his eyes and breathed deeply. Pa had been kneeling by him, offering words of encouragement, but now he recognised that he was trying to focus. Silence fell between them, despite the noise and general chaos around them.

Mitch walked into the room first, guided only by the small screen of his night vision camera. The room seemed to be still and silent. As he crossed the threshold, Mark reached the point of spiritual perfection. In a swift and unexpected movement, he kicked out with his right leg. The ball in front of him flew across the room and bounced at the feet of the team.

Silence filled the room as the ball came to a halt. Then the spirits all cheered and fell onto Mark, hugging him and congratulating him. Then Thomas put Mark up on his shoulders and took him on a victory lap around the house, shouting to all who could hear him about the amazing feat this baby had just accomplished.

"Mark threw the ball at the team! They got it on camera!" Everyone came out of their rooms to marvel at his talents and achievements. Mark beamed from ear to ear as he was kissed, cuddled and patted on the back by one and all. He had done the impossible and he had done it with style. For years to come, this moment would be remembered as the team's best evidence. And it would be referred to and watched repeatedly on YouTube, clocking up over a million views in a very short time. If only the viewers knew who had moved the ball! Most were amazed by the sudden, explosive nature of the movement, but knowing that it was achieved by a baby would have shocked them to their core.

Shaken by this evidence, the team lingered for a short while, asking questions to the apparently empty room, but got no response. They checked the voice recorder on the table then left to check the other rooms.

After the team had left, the ghosts decided that they needed Claire. Nat went to fetch her from the dining room without telling her what was planned for her. Once she was in the room, she was pounced on by a number of ghosts, who started to tickle her and blow raspberries on her stomach. Claire quickly realised that she was in no danger, but those who were tickling her were. In between the laughter and giggles, her limbs flailed and struck out at anyone within range. Unwittingly, she kicked Ethan in the face and caught Pa in the groin. All too soon, Claire was laughing in victory and rolling on the floor with the others that she had somehow taken out. If their laughter wasn't heard by the team, then nothing ever would be.

Nat knew what Claire was like when she was being tickled, so he stood back and watched as she floored all of those around her. Now he joined his love on the floor and kissed her first on her belly then her lips, both of them smiling. "You monster!" Claire said quietly to him.

"I know you can take care of yourself, and you do have a great laugh," replied Nat as he continued to kiss her. Around them the others were still giggling, hugging and trying to get up off the floor.

"I will never tickle another person in my death. Especially you!" said Pa as he rolled over and hugged Claire and Nat. "Your girlfriend is savage!"

The investigation team had moved away from the stillness of the library and had gone straight down to the cellar. Here they sat in silence and waited for something to happen. The house was so active, they knew it was just a matter of time before something else happened. With all this activity, how could the current owners live here? Surely they were being bombarded on a daily basis. Yet they had made no mention of anything like this. Was this all a set-up? If so, how was it being achieved? Or was it their presence that had induced the spirits to put on this show?

Jonas couldn't stop thinking. He sat silently in the darkness of the old kitchen with the rest of the team. They were all stunned by this seemingly quiet country house. They had investigated all sorts of places before, but never anything like this. In a pub in Somerset they had been thrown and verbally abused by a demonic entity. In an average three-bed semi, one of them had been burned and cut by another demon. Despite these experiences, they had been unprepared for this. Everything they had witnessed was non-violent except for the first spirit box session. Could that have been a wind-up? Do ghosts have a sense of humour?

Jonas's train of thought was brought to a sudden halt as he heard something metal bounce on the floor right in front of him. While the team sat in the dark, pondering everything that they had witnessed, the master had come in and stopped the ghosts there.

"I completely forgot about these," the master said as he handed John a handful of old coins.

"What are they?" asked Simon.

"Coins. Old coins. No idea where they keep coming from, but I've yet to meet a ghost that can't hold them. I thought they would be good to throw. Easier than trying to make our footsteps heard."

In the dim light of the cellar, Simon looked long and hard at the coins in his hand. All were so old that they would have been out of circulation for years. Simon, Felicia, William, Stan and Elle spaced themselves out in the room. William threw first. Jonas jumped to his feet and put his torch on to find the source of the noise and movement. There at his feet was a shiny penny.

"What is it?" asked Phil.

"It's a penny. Hold the light so I can read the date. 1903," replied Jonas.

"That's old. Could we have knocked it?" questioned Mitch as he took hold of the penny and examined it himself. "It's warm!"

"I know, I thought that. Any ideas?" said Jonas.

Ian turned from the team and addressed the darkness. "Do you have any more for us?"

Simon tossed a coin into the air. It bounced several times before coming to a halt on the floor by the door.

"Thank you. Keep them coming!"

"Got it, it's another penny. This one's warm as well. What's going on?" asked Phil, as the sound of something rolling along the ground caught his attention.

"It's rare, but I have heard of this. Happy spirits can manifest coins. No one knows why, but that's what's happened in the past," explained Ian. Another coin hit the ground. This one was thrown by Elle. Her aim wasn't that good, as it nearly hit Phil on the back of his head. Luckily it wasn't until it hit the ground that he realised it was in his vicinity. With each penny thrown, the team and the assembled ghosts got more and more excited. Ghosts and living alike were all trying to spot where the last penny had rolled or bounced to. Torchlight bounced all over the place as they tried to hunt this amazing quarry.

All too soon the ghosts had exhausted their supply of coins. Yet the team continued to search, desperate to find them all.

"Are we all out?" asked William, a broad smile on his face.

"Pennies from heaven! How many have we got?" Jonas smiled as he counted up the coins in his hand. "I've got seven."

"Six," said Phil.

"I've got nine," said Ian.

"And I've got seven too!" replied Mitch.

"That sounds like all of them," said William, as he looked round at the ghosts and their empty hands.

"Did you count them before?" Stan asked the master.

"No, I didn't think. But that does sound about right. That's another highlight for them, despite what they called me and Pa."

Slowly the team began to calm down. Ian had heard of this phenomenon, but none of them had actually witnessed it. Jonas had already decided that they would have to come back to this amazing house one day. This house was the paranormal world's equivalent of the Grand Canyon or the hanging gardens of Babylon – a wonder that all could appreciate, regardless of their background or opinion.

The team were exhausted; it had been a long night. With dawn just a few hours away, they decided to do one last experiment. They headed back to the library. Mitch switched on the lights so they could set up the table and chairs for this last act. With darkness restored, the team sat around the table. All the ghosts had also assembled, and were packed into the room. Before it was large and spacious, now it was cramped and full. The table was round and quite large. In between the seated team four ghosts stood, waiting for them to begin.

Jonas looked around at the camera. "Right, this is our last experiment. It's called table tipping. If you're a fan of the show, you will have seen us do this before. Since we seem to have so many spirits around us, this should work well. You can see under the table, and you should be able to see that we are not touching the table at all. Are we all ready? Fingers touching, please, and we will see if they can move this table."

Around them Simon, Martin, Claire and Stan took hold of the table edge.

"We give you permission to use our energy. Please can you move this table for us?" continued Jonas, his eyes closed to everything around him as he focused on the task at hand.

"Ready? One, two, three, lift!" instructed the master, who stood behind them. All four ghosts lifted, putting all their strength into it. But the table might as well have been welded to the floor. After a few seconds of extreme strain, the table moved a few millimetres.

"It moved!" shouted Jonas. "You've got it, keep it going!"

The four spirits couldn't do any more; they were exhausted. So the master gave the nod and they stepped away from their positions and allowed another four ghosts to step up and test their strength.

Pa, John, Elle and Ethan stepped forward, and waited for the count.

"One, two, three, lift!" shouted the master. With every sinew of their beings, they heaved. The table began to slowly move. Quickly the investigation team stood and pushed their chairs out of the way. Then they too began to move with the table, as it twisted across the floor.

"This is amazing, you're doing it. Please keep it going!" exclaimed Phil, as the others marvelled at this latest feat of supernatural power.

Pa suddenly buckled under the strain. His legs wobbled, and Simon had to help him out of the way. The others followed suit, without argument. They had given it everything they had. Now the room spun, and their legs felt like lead. Exhaustion and physical pain was evident on their faces.

The next four ghosts faced up to the table. Nat cracked his knuckles, while Thomas stretched out his arms. Then when they, Chloe and another young man from the city had positioned themselves around the table, they lifted as one, all of them breathing hard as they tried to move the impossible. The table was just starting to shift when Nat screamed and winced in pain. Cramp was tearing at his arms, and he was unable to continue. In fairness, he had done a lot that night, and his energy levels were beginning to fade.

Finally it was William's turn. He, Felicia, Bill and Alan braced themselves. Then, with a nod from William, they gave it all they could. The table started to move. Once more its subtle movement was given away by the sound of the table's feet scraping on the floor. The four ghosts looked at each other as they forced themselves even more. The table continued to scratch across the wooden floor. With every inch the investigation team became more and more excited.

"This is amazing!" they shouted. "I can't believe you're doing this!"

But the ghosts couldn't keep it going forever. William could feel his back going, despite fighting as hard as he could. Pain stopped him in his tracks and he collapsed onto the table, his hands still gripping its edge.

The master looked around at the room full of spent spirits. "Anyone else want another go?"

Most shook their heads or waved their hands in objection. William was still flat out on the table. All he could muster was, "Fuck, I think my back's gone."

Claire and Martin peeled him off the table and laid him down on the floor to recover. Mark, who had been in a corner out of the way, now set about checking on the ghosts. They were all exhausted. No one was going to try again; that was obvious. Yet everyone was laughing and smiling. Tiredness had given way to joy and happiness.

The investigation team were also done for the night. The table-tipping experiment had sapped the last of their energy. The excitement of the evening's events had kept them going longer than they should have, but now the living sun was beginning to creep back into the world they could barely stand, let alone think. Slumped in a chair, Jonas began to address his audience. "Well, that was amazing! We have had the best night here in rural Bechford. We could not have predicted all of tonight's activity. But that can, and does, happen. This is the end of our time here so, until next time, it's goodbye from all of us. Tune in next time to see what goes bump in the night at the Old Prison, Birmingham." With that Jonas's head dropped and he muttered something about needing sleep.

Only two souls remained standing at the end of this amazing night, the master and Mark. Both were delighted with how it had all gone, and their own personal achievements. Yet even they were tired and needed a rest.

The master slowly lowered himself to the floor. Some of the ghosts were still breathing deeply, while others, like William and Nat, nursed their sore spots. However, none of them had stopped smiling. They had done the impossible, and that made them all feel amazing!

Slowly the investigation team and the spirits around them began to move. The team headed back to the monitors and started to turn off the recording equipment. The ghosts, in groups of two or three, headed to the stream, in urgent need of replenishment.

The last to leave were the master, Pa and Jonas. The three of them watched as the sky changed colour, revealing a new day and the end of a spectacular night. Watching the sun rise after being up all night is very different to getting up early enough to witness this daily event. The colours are the same, so is the sound of the dawn chorus. Yet when you have been up all night, dawn feels and looks different somehow, as if you are looking at it from the wrong side. Either way, the three men enjoyed this moment together and in silence until The master suddenly said, "I know how to get even. He did call us both demons, so he needs putting right. Are you in?"

"Of course! What have you in mind?" Pa rubbed his chin and smiled broadly. He stood up and walked towards the dining room. The master had an idea of what Pa had planned and followed, rubbing his hands with glee. This would be another naughty but nice moment. The trigger objects and camera were still in place. Jonas had said he would turn off the camera, then head back to the others. The two men stood and watched as Jonas entered and did as he had intended. He stopped and looked at the two objects, which had both clearly moved: the Bible most of all. He would check the footage later with the others, just to make sure it hadn't been the cat. It wasn't the cat; the team of ghosts had managed to move both without feline assistance. With the camera off, Jonas turned around to leave the room. Instead of an empty room, he was faced by two strange men. One in old-fashioned clothes, but nevertheless smart and clearly military, going by his stance. The other was larger and the dead spit of Father Christmas. To say that Jonas's heart skipped a beat would be an understatement.

"You said that we were demonic entities. As you can see, we are not. That might get you on the naughty list. Next time, don't assume. We know you can do better," said Pa, then with his traditional "Ho, ho, ho" the two ghosts faded from view, and burst out laughing. Jonas was as white as a sheet, yet he was full of excitement and wonder.

"Sorry, er, Santa," he said to the empty space in front of him. The two ghosts were holding their sides, which were sore with laughing. Jonas was stunned. He had seen a ghost from a distance before, but not like this. This was something else.

There were two cameras in this room, one facing the trigger objects and one attached to the wall, giving a perfect overall view of the room. But they were both off; the green light that said they were on and recording had been replaced by a red light, indicating standby mode.

Without proof, who would believe him? It was such an unusual encounter that he struggled to comprehend it himself. As he stood there, he soon came to the conclusion that even his team would doubt it, so he would keep it to himself. Yet he had just been told off by Santa. That thought would guide him for years – after all, who wants to be on the naughty list? Jonas, outside the investigations, became a model of good behaviour and generosity. Gone were the bad habits of his youth, replaced by voluntary work and donations to various charities. That he had met the real Santa would not be revealed until he himself had children, when he confessed his shock and wonder at this glorious encounter with the man himself.

The master and Pa left the confused Jonas, laughing fit to bust.

"That will take him down a peg or two!" giggled the master, as they left the house and headed towards the stream, where the others had gathered.

As they got closer, they could hear laughter and chatting as various people recounted their night. Despite their tiredness, the high from tonight would last for weeks. Along the stream the spirits had settled in small groups, but with little space in between, giving the place the feeling of a family get-together. Everyone was sitting or lying down, trying to rest their bodies, while their emotions soared.

After around half an hour of this Nat and Claire stood up, holding hands. "We think that now is a good time to tell you all that we are engaged!" said Nat proudly. En masse, the ghosts rushed to congratulate the beautiful couple on their good news. "Of course, you are all invited to the wedding, but we don't know where to find a vicar."

"Not a problem, lad, we know one. When do you want to do the deed?" asked Bill as he shook Nat's hand warmly.

"Soonish, we think," replied Claire as she hugged Bill.

"Well, give us a day or two to get over tonight and we will be happy to go and get him for you," said Bill, exchanging smiles with Elle and Alan.

Now the mood had gone through the roof! In the melee of spirits hugging and congratulating the happy couple, no one noticed Mark. He sat quietly, slightly away from the others. As the crowd began to settle down, Mark crawled towards Nat and Claire. Nat saw him and joined Mark on the floor, ready to greet him. But before he could say anything or hug him, Mark put something in his hand. Then Mark's tiny hands wrapped around Nat's, closing it and sealing it with a kiss. Nat had been a rocker in his day, and showing emotion was not his strong point. But before he looked at what was in his hand, he rubbed the baby's face gently, a warm smile on his face. Tears would have been shed if he been alive. Claire spotted this delicate moment and joined Nat and Mark on the ground.

Slowly Nat opened his hand to reveal a perfect daisy-chain ring. Nat and Claire were amazed that Mark could have produced something so beautiful. Around them the spirits had fallen silent. Mark sat smiling at them both. His eyes glistened but no tears fell.

Nat took the ring and placed it on Claire's ring finger, then they kissed to the sound of cheers and whoops from the crowd. Mark's tokens were always special, but this was achingly perfect.

Chapter 33

The date had been set: All Saints Day. Ghosts came from far and wide for the reception the day before, and the ceremony. The priest had spoken to Nat and Claire, but this was a premarital talk with a difference. He was clear about the risks of getting married in the spirit world.

When the dead marry, it is a lottery. Sometimes the vows are said, and the ceremony ends like that in the world of the living, with the couple kissing and the crowd cheering and clapping. What Nat and Claire hoped for, as did their family, was that they would kiss and move on together. The most common outcome was far more dangerous: that one of them would move on, leaving the other heartbroken and stuck, which as we all know can lead to addiction to negative emotions.

Everyone prayed that they would either move on or stay together. The prospect of one of them being left behind wasn't discussed or even mentioned, except by the priest. But the former monk turned priest couldn't, and wouldn't, sugar-coat it for them. He had seen what happens when marriage goes wrong, and it was never pretty.

Because of the possible ending to the ceremony, it is traditional in the ghost world to hold the reception the day before the wedding, just in case. And should the couple remain, they can party with friends and family both before and after.

As luck would have it, the Friday before was when "their" episode of *Mostly Ghostly* was due to be aired. Nat knew that William would want to watch it at his house, so he could keep an eye on Sarah's reaction. Claire and the others would watch it at the town hall, along with dozens of the living residents of Bechford.

William and Nat sat cross-legged in front of the TV in the front room, keen to get the best view of their antics. As the family around them jumped or gasped in shock, the two ghosts giggled, remembering what had really happened. Claire had been heard clearly. Nat flatly commented, "If we both stay, she might just kill me for letting that happen."

"I doubt it. She's too smart for that. But you might want to watch your back, she's cunning and clever!" replied William with a giggle.

All too soon, Jonas was standing outside the manor house, preparing to close the show. "We have had the best night here! Even without using high-tech equipment, we have got some amazing evidence.

The owners were blown away by what has happened tonight. This house is haunted, but I wonder if the spirits came out in force for us. It felt like it. Following our night here we can only conclude that, in this house, it's not just those who died here who haunt it. There are others that are connected to this beautiful building in some way. We are so grateful to them all. We will be back to the manor house, Bechford. Until then, on behalf of all of us, we wish you all a happy Halloween!"

With that the credits rolled, then there was an advert for the horror film that would follow.

"We did it! I wonder how long it will be before they come back?" asked William.

"Only a few years, I guess. If we're still here, we will be able to do all that again!" replied Nat.

"No, we will have to do better. I can see a lot of time spent practising with the master." William smiled. Behind them Sarah, Oliver and Luke sat in silence, unsure what they had just witnessed. The family wouldn't have faked any of that, never mind all of it.

"Right, I think it's safe to leave this lot to their own devices. Shall we get going? The club will be packed tonight!" William said. With a nod of agreement, the two ghosts got up and walked out of the house. A comfortable silence fell between them. They had been walking for several minutes before Nat broke it. "Just in case…"

"Don't go there, you'll both be fine," replied William.

"No, mate. I need to know what is in that pouch of yours. It's been bugging me for ages!" Nat smiled.

William burst out laughing. "You wait until now to ask me? Why wait? Idiot!"

"Because I assumed it was private or weird. With us, I can never tell which it will be," said Nat.

The two stopped and William carefully opened the pouch that hung from his belt and emptied the contents into his hand.

"I used to keep bits and pieces in it, but when I died, my parents and brother emptied it and put something in it from each of them. The flowers are from my mother – she loved having flowers around the house. The horse was a good luck charm."

"It's lost a leg!"

"I know. I broke it by accident when I was little. My dad convinced me that he would take bad luck for me. Not that he would ward off bad luck, just that bad luck would hit him, not me."

"The horse is a he?"

"Of course it is. It was part of a pair and the other was small, so this one was the stallion."

"And the coin?"

"My brother took what money I had and drank it. But he gave me this in return." Between his thumb and finger, William held up the coin so that Nat could see it properly. Because William had been buried with these things, he could, at will, hold on to them, but others might struggle. The coin was a mint bezant. "The gold ones were more common. You saw them everywhere, even though they were technically illegal tender. But John got this one working for the smithy."

The small silver coin almost glowed in the bright daylight as William and Nat looked at it.

Carefully William placed the three sacred items back into his pouch and pulled the string tight to secure it. "See, nothing weird or really private, just a bit random. Like us, I suppose!"

Nat smiled at his brother in death and patted him on the back. They then continued towards the club.

By the time Nat and William arrived, the party was in full swing, for both living and dead revellers. It was Halloween, so most were in fancy dress. The large group of ghosts spent the night dancing, singing and celebrating what was to come later. At first the priest was reluctant to join in, but Claire was having none of it. She grabbed his hand and pulled him onto the dance floor. In a short time, he was smiling and dancing with the others. None of them seemed out of place tonight, except Pa. Having danced with everyone, including a slow dance with Claire, he decided that the best thing to do would be to stand near the loos. He was visible to the living one minute and gone the next. It was very confusing for the living who smiled or said hello to him, then watched as he vanished before their eyes. Felicia heard one young man tell his friends that he thought someone had spiked his drink, because he had seen something odd, but wouldn't reveal what. Just that it was too strange to discuss!

At about 3.50 a.m. the lights in the club came on and the music was switched off. This was the sign that they were closing and it was time to go home. For the dead, this meant it was time to go to the church.

Ethan and Tom led the procession into the church. The priest took his place in front of the altar. William stood proudly next to Nat as he nervously combed his fingers through his hair. Besides them sat Mark, who had spent the last few days in the garden. He had crafted another – and in his mind, better – wedding ring. The priest had taken it and kept it safe inside his vestments. Now Mark carefully held it ready to present at the right time. Outside, Claire went around to the graveyard with Felicia, Elle and the master. Having spent the night dancing, her hair required some tidying, and she needed a moment to compose herself.

The church was packed with ghosts. They all sat in the pews anxiously waiting for the bride-to-be. Outside it was a bright spring day for the dead. Light streamed through the stained-glass windows. Random patches of colour decorated the space within, creating a beautiful mosaic of light and colour; there was no need for flowers.

The master put his hand through the main door to indicate to the priest that they were ready. The priest raised his hands and the congregation rose together and started to hum or sing 'Here Comes the Bride'. The priest had known someone that was able to play the organ or piano, but they had moved on several years before, so it was back to basics. With so many working together the music sounded surprisingly good, despite the number of ghosts who were totally tone deaf.

Arm in arm, the master escorted Claire down the aisle, her maid of honour and bridesmaid following. Nat fought the urge to turn around. Even in the spirit realm, it is bad luck to look at the bride before she takes her place next to her groom.

"Dearly beloved, we are gathered here in the sight of God and this congregation to witness the joining of these two souls in holy matrimony. Who brings this woman to be wed?" began the priest.

"I do," said the master, as he kissed Claire on the cheek then handed Claire's hand to Nat.

"Is there any soul here that has just cause or impediment why these two should not be joined? Speak now or forever hold your peace," said the priest.

Silence filled the church. Nervously Nat looked round at the congregation, but no one objected. Only smiles and tears of joy greeted Nat's eyes.

"Good, I always dread that bit! Claire, you know the vows?"

Claire smiled at the priest then turned to face Nat. Her smile widened as she looked into the eyes of her beloved. "I, Claire Ann Thomson, take thee, Nathan George Simmons, to be my wedded husband. To have and to hold from this day forward, for better or worse, in sickness and in health, I bind my soul to yours for all time. To love and to cherish, honour and obey, in this life and the next. According to God's holy ordinance, and thereto I pledge myself to you." Claire breathed out deeply and her hands shook in Nat's firm but gentle grip.

"Mark, do you have the ring?" said the priest. Mark stood, wobbling slightly, and handed this most treasured of creations to Nat. Nat bent down and kissed Mark on the forehead. No words were needed, then with a smile at William he turned back to Claire.

Placing the ring on Claire's finger, Nat repeated the vows. "I, Nathan George Simmons, take thee, Claire Ann Thomson, to be my wedded wife. To have and to hold from this day forward, for better or worse, in sickness and in health, I bind my soul to yours for all time. To love and to cherish, honour and obey, in this life and the next. According to God's holy ordinance and thereto I pledge myself to you." He too was relieved that the vows were over; he had spent days memorising them. William patted his brother on the back and stood back. Smiling at Claire, he winked, then bent down and picked up Mark. Claire and Nat stopped and looked at her hand and the ring that bound them together forever.

"With the giving of a ring and the exchange of vows, said in front of God and these your family and friends, I declare that you are now husband and wife. You may kiss your bride," said the priest, but unlike the master, William and Mark he did not stand back.

The couple kissed deep and long, to the rapturous applause of all that were there. After a second or two, the couple began to glow. Still in a deep embrace, the gentle glow intensified until the light was so bright that no one could look directly at them. Then with a loud boom, they disappeared from view. The force of the blast shook the building, causing the bells to ring without warning. They had moved on together.

As the ghosts that remained got back to their feet, cheers and celebrations broke out. Spirits hugged each other and cried tears of joy. Heartbroken and happy, people began to notice the sweet smell of freshly cut flowers. The smell wasn't overpowering, but it was there. This smell was noticeable to the living for many days, in and around the church. For the dead, the aroma could be detected for several miles around the church, and for more than a few days!

The feeling of pure joy that this wonderful couple had emitted filled the hearts of all the ghosts who had witnessed this perfect passing. The celebrations that followed would be forever remembered by those spirits. There was dancing in the streets, singing and laughter. Grief was not even considered. Yes, they had lost two dear friends, but they had left this existence filled with love and had moved on to the next together.

Chapter 34

Several months had passed since Nat and Claire had moved on together. Since then, daily death had returned to normal. William was encouraged, but still slightly nervous about Sarah, who had been spending her spare time researching the family tree.

Despite her extensive search, she hadn't found a single Claire in her ancestry. A Claire had spoken through Harriet, so Sarah assumed that she and Claire must be related, but she wasn't. Sarah had, however, found out about her great-grandfather's role in the Great War, and her six times great-grandmother who had run away to join the circus. Sarah had even found a spectacular pamphlet describing her as the Lion Lady of Lincoln!

Now she was secretly visiting places that her mother had known. It wasn't hard to visit Amber's school, as Amber and Luke had met when they attended the same secondary school as Sarah and Oliver now went to. Going to her mother's primary school had meant a bus journey, but that was no real hassle.

Amber and her sister Paige had spent their early years on an estate about twenty miles away. Sarah had her heart set on visiting her ancestral home. William had heard Sarah and her friend Emily organising when they would go. Emily didn't need any encouragement; she had just got her first car, and she grabbed any excuse to drive with both hands. Felicia and Mark were also keen to visit this fabled town. Anyway, it was a good reason to take a day trip.

On the morning of the planned jaunt, however, Emily had to cancel. Her beloved car had failed to start, and not for the first time. So, the bus would have to do. Sarah had to catch two buses to get close to her desired destination. Sarah didn't mind having to go by herself; she had set her heart on visiting that house today, and she was going to fulfil that ambition.

Sarah's bus stopped a short walk from the house. She stepped off the bus, followed by William, Felicia and Mark. On the way there the three ghosts didn't see many other ghosts, but that was not unusual. For the dead it was the middle of the night, whereas for the living it was just after lunch.

The walk from the bus stop to the house was not a comfortable one for any of the intrepid day-trippers. The area had become poor and had lost all hope with the closure of the factory that had once employed most of the local population. Sarah could see degradation and crime all around her. Many of the houses were boarded up with metal sheets, piles of rubbish littered the ground, and graffiti seemed to be on every square inch of wall. Sarah felt very uncomfortable. She didn't know any of the faces that she passed, and it was obvious from the looks they gave her that she did not belong here.

Outside the house, Sarah stopped and pulled out an old photo. Felicia and William leaned over Sarah's shoulder to look at it with her.

"That's her grandparents, that's her mother, Amber, that's her aunt, Paige, and I can't remember the name of the dog. Sorry," said William as he pointed to the various faces on the worn image.

The house in the picture was a pretty, well-maintained three-bed semi, seemingly overflowing with hope and happiness. Sadly, that house was long gone. The building remained, but the home was no more. The windows were boarded up, there was a large hole in the roof, and the manicured garden had vanished beneath the jungle that now engulfed the property.

"Right, now you've seen it, we can go. Before you get into trouble!" said William as he looked around nervously. But his wisdom fell on deaf ears. Sarah was driven on by curiosity. She moved slowly through the garden and round to the back of the property. Brambles grabbed at Sarah's clothes, slowing her progress, but her determination drove her on. To the ghosts' dismay the back door had been removed and thrown into the deep undergrowth that hid the large back garden from view.

"Hello, anyone home?" Sarah called through the open doorway, but there was no response.

Clean sunlight hit the grime of the inside. Through the doorway Sarah could see what remained of the kitchen. There were missing cupboard doors and no running water, but at least she could recognise that it had once been a working kitchen. The three spirits followed Sarah as she walked into the lounge-diner. It was a large space, but very dark, despite the bright daylight. The metal sheets that protected the property had small holes to allow air movement, but they weren't sufficient to let real light in. Sarah reached into her bag, pulled out her phone and started to take photos. The flash of the camera lit up the room for a brief second, revealing more than you might want to see. There was an old sofa and a broken chair, but no other furniture. Rubbish had collected in piles around the space. Used needles and dead candles seemed to be everywhere Sarah pointed her phone. The house had once been a home, but recently it had sadly become a drugs den.

Slowly Sarah made her way past the front door and up the bare wooden stairs, using the light on her phone as a torch. Upstairs the darkness was less, but still ever present. The first door she looked through was to the bathroom – or rather, it had been. Tiles had been pulled off the walls; the sink and toilet had been smashed. The only thing that remained was the enamel bath. Sarah looked round the door. She could see the shattered pieces of porcelain that littered the floor and the bath, along with a thick layer of dirt that covered everything.

Next Sarah checked the boxroom. In the gloom all she could make out was a collection of rubbish. Quickly she moved on to the master bedroom. Through a crack she could see out to the street outside. The hustle and bustle outside was a stark contrast to the stillness and quiet of the interior of the house. In the master bedroom was an old mattress that looked – and smelled – as if someone – or something – had died on it, along with piles of discarded rubbish and needles.

It was so silent and still. Sarah reached into her bag once more. This time she pulled out a voice recorder. She passed slowly up and down the room, asking questions of this abused space. William, Felicia and Mark could see even less than Sarah, but had nevertheless followed her carefully. They attempted to respond to her enquiries, but they weren't heard. After a few minutes Sarah headed to the second bedroom, which had once been her mother's room. The door opened with little effort, revealing light. The sheeting on the outside of the window had slipped, allowing light to penetrate this room at least. Sarah headed straight for the window. She placed the recorder down as she breathed in the clean air that came in through a broken pane. William followed her to the window. For him the light of the new moon was next to useless, but at least it wasn't cloudy.

"William. Behind you!" shouted Felicia as she quickly backed into the corner with Mark. William turned and saw, to his shock, a man standing there, holding something. In the gloom it was difficult to tell what it was. But this was not a good situation. Behind him, Sarah looked out of the window, oblivious to this turn of events. Then she caught sight of the man's reflection and turned quickly to meet his gaze. He was clearly homeless and scared. Before Sarah could explain what she was doing, he lunged at her. His blade tore into flesh, but it wasn't Sarah's. William had held his ground: now the knife had sliced into his body.

Shock and blind panic filled the room. Sarah and her would-be attacker could see William now. William's love for Sarah had caused him to fully manifest – not just as a solid shape, but as flesh and blood. The man pulled the knife out and ran for his life. William collapsed backwards into Sarah. As they fell, her arms wrapped round his limp body.

"Just hold on, I'll call an ambulance," said Sarah as she looked for her phone.

"Don't bother. I'm William, you live in my old house. We've been trying to tell you to stop looking for your mother. She didn't stay, I'm sorry," said William.

Sarah could see the wound to his stomach and the seemingly endless flow of blood. She pushed down hard on the wound, trying to stem the flow, but it wasn't working. She didn't know this man, yet she was crying for him.

"Just hold on, you'll be fine," said Sarah, reassuring this man as much as herself. William looked towards Felicia and Mark, who had joined them on the floor. Their eyes glistened with tears that refused to flow, yet there was also the hint of happiness.

"Tell the others I love them all, and I'll see you all soon," he said as he held Felicia's hand. Mark leaned forward and kissed his blood-soaked hand, his eyes red with emotion.

With his other hand, William reached round to caress Sarah's face. The fear and despair on her face was plain to see, as she couldn't see Felicia or Mark.

"These are Felicia and Mark. They will keep an eye on you, because you are family now, and we all love you, and your brother and father." With that, his hand dropped and William fell silent, then he began to glow. He glowed brighter and brighter until both living and dead had to shield their eyes from the glare. When the light was almost too much to bear, it was gone … and so was William.

Sarah hadn't moved, yet the body and blood had disappeared. Sarah could still feel the sticky warmth of the blood on her hands and body, but there was no sign of it.

Panic set in. In one swift movement she got up and ran out of the empty room. Halfway down the stairs, she realised she had left her phone behind. Cautiously she climbed the stairs and re-entered the room. Checking behind the door this time, she made sure it was empty. She picked up her phone and the voice recorder off the windowsill, then hurried out of the house.

Sarah ran at full pelt back to the presumed safety of the bus stop. She shook with fear all the way home, but she held it together until she stepped into the sanctuary of her own bedroom and closed the door behind her. Then her legs buckled, and she dropped to the floor. Sarah crawled to her bed and let her eyes close.

Sarah woke a few hours later. The sun was still shining, but clouds were starting to move in. Fearfully she plugged her headphones into the voice recorder and turned up the volume.

"Just hold on, you'll be fine," Sarah said clearly on the recording.

"Tell the others I love them all, and I'll see you all soon." William's voice was clear and easy to hear, but impossible to forget...

Dedication

This book is dedicated to the memory of my father. It was while I was caring for my father in his final weeks that I started writing this book. *Love From Beyond* was my only escape from the horror of watching my wonderful father fade to nothing. My dad was clever, supportive and kind to a fault. I'm glad he isn't suffering any more, but I wish he had lived to see this book published.

Losing my dad nearly broke me. I hope this book and its nicer characters will provide some comfort to readers who are also grieving. If you are struggling, I urge you to ask for help.

Below are some organisations that can help you through the dark days and nights.

At a Loss – www.ataloss.org

Child Bereavement UK – 0800 028 8840, www.childbereavementuk.org

The Compassionate Friends – 0345 123 2304, www.tcf.org.uk

Dying Matters – www.dyingmatters.org

The Good Grief Trust – www.thegoodgrieftrust.org

Samaritans – 116 123 (freephone)

Sands – 0808 164 3332

Sudden – 0800 2600 400, www.sudden.org

Widowed and Young (WAY) – www.widowedandyoung.org.uk

Printed in Dunstable, United Kingdom